E. Lee

Those Darn Dithers

Those Darn Dithers

SID HITE

Henry Holt and Company

New York

For my nieces
Allie, Amy, Casandra, Cecelia, Jade,
Jill, Rayna, Valerie

Henry Holt and Company, Inc.
Publishers since 1866
115 West 18th Street
New York, New York 10011

Henry Holt is a registered
trademark of Henry Holt and Company, Inc.
Copyright © 1996 by Sid Hite
All rights reserved.
Published in Canada by Fitzhenry & Whiteside Ltd.,
195 Allstate Parkway, Markham, Ontario L3R 4T8.

Library of Congress Cataloging-in-Publication Data
Hite, Sid.
    Those darn Dithers / Sid Hite.
        p.   cm.
    Summary: This sequel to *Dither Farm* continues the antics of the Dither family
and their quirky neighbors in Willow County, Virginia.
    [1. Family life—Virginia—Fiction   2. Country life—Virginia—Fiction.
3. Virginia—Fiction.]   I. Title.
PZ7.H62964Th   1996   [Fic]—dc20   96-22400

ISBN 0-8050-3838-8
First Edition—1996
Designed by Martha Rago
Printed in the United States of America on acid-free paper. ∞
10 9 8 7 6 5 4 3 2 1

Few things will wake you up quicker than a brisk dance with mortality. It revitalizes the senses and reminds you that you are lucky to breathe.

—*The Comprehensive Guide*

Clementine and Henry Dither	*Sweethearts since high school.* *They have five kids.*
Holly Dither, 14	*Wants to be a big star*
Emmet Dither, 13	*An aspiring vaudevillian*
Matilda Dither, 12	*A thinker and a reader*
Archibald Dither, 9	*A busybody*
Angeline Dither, 1 ½	*A born singer*
Emma A. Bean	*Clementine's mysterious aunt.* *A parapsychologist, she's mar-* *ried to Leopold Hillacre.*
Leopold Hillacre	*Elderly eccentric, philosopher,* *and writer*
Carl Plummers	*A very big man and a fixture* *in Aylor's Store*
Stella Plummers	*Carl's deceased twin sister*
Jimmy Aylor	*Proud owner of Aylor's Store*
Alice Aylor	*Jimmy's accordion-playing* *wife*
Flea Jenfries	*Clementine's dearest friend* *and Warren's legal guardian*
Warren Robinson, 14	*Emmet's best friend. He's* *sweet on Holly.*
Garland Barlow	*Local mechanic and welder* *who was "bit by a Flea"*

Acorn and Bart	*Two brothers rescued from a life of crime by Garland*
Contessa Cunningham, 13	*The apple of Emmet's eye*
Mike Cunningham	*Contessa's father, a magician*
Beaufort B. Beaumont, 16	*Holly's handsome costar at Queen's Playland*
Sally Swope	*Director of the Wild West Show*
Marvin Jinks	*An old acquaintance of Henry's, now a literary agent in New York City*

Nonhuman characters

Senator	*Emmet's monkey*
Rosey	*Mike Cunningham's monkey*
Dan	*Holly's show pony*
Goosebumps	*Matilda's lazy mutt*
Porcellina	*Contessa's dancing pig*

Close friends of the Dither family

Millie Ross
Bellamonte Smoot

Local Color

Wade Butcher
Felton Fibbs
Sheriff Ludwell Newton
Eugenna White

Those Darn Dithers

Part One

Chapter One

It was a warm, wet morning in Willow County, and the world was enveloped by a dense fog that dimmed the sun and obscured all but the most prominent features of the land. This ghostly blanket had been born after four days and nights of incessant rain. The rain had stopped, but the air was as clammy as wet diapers and the sky as gray as the bark on a sycamore tree. When the wind blew, it sloshed instead of whirred. Hydrologists had a field day. Everywhere the earth was either flooded or so waterlogged it bubbled underfoot.

It was a Wednesday morning in early June. Plants flopped sideways in the mud, drunken slugs lay exposed on the open ground, nervous cows herded together on soggy hilltops, sheep flocked onto wet knolls, dogs cowered under damp porches, and all feathered vertebrates ascended the troposphere in search of dryness. Dampness ruled the world.

Humans retreated into white clapboard houses to bask under the glare of electric lights. A practical few wore bathing suits while others wrapped towels around their heads. Frightened children called to Chicken Little: The sky has fallen on Willow County, and the clouds are stuck to the ground.

Although it was impossible to see the side of a barn from twenty feet away and anyone walking outdoors ran the risk of smacking into a tree, or worse, one brave individual prepared to venture into the phantasmic mist. His name was Archibald Dither. He was nine years old.

Archibald's mother caught him slipping out the back door. "Where do you think you're going?"

"Out."

"Out?" Clementine replied. "Are you nuts? You'll be lost out there in no time!"

After four days of domestic confinement Archibald felt as though the walls of the house were crashing in on him. "So what if I do get lost?" he said lightheartedly. "I'll find my way home eventually."

Clementine sighed and ran a hand through her thick black hair. "Arch, you could fall in a ditch and no one would know to come look for you."

Archibald shrugged. He could think of worse fates. "I've fallen in ditches before. Got out all by myself."

Clementine struggled to keep from smiling.

Archibald could see that his mother's resolve was weakening. "There's nothing to do in the house," he explained. "I've read all of Matilda's books, the TV is dead, and I've played so much Fish the cards are wet. And besides, I'm tired of listening to Holly harp about the big contract she signed at Queen's Playland."

"Holly is excited about Queen's Playland," Clementine

replied tersely. "And she has every right to be. Instead of begrudging her success, you should be proud of your sister."

"Sorry," Archibald said with a shrug. "I wasn't trying to begrudge anyone. I just want to go out."

Clementine crossed her arms and hemmed.

"Pretty please. I haven't seen Carl for four days."

Clementine sighed and softened her stance. Carl Plummers and Jimmy Aylor had met when they served in the Navy together during World War Two. Soon after the conflict ended, Carl had visited Willow County, and now, two decades later, he was still visiting. Clementine knew that Archibald and Carl were best friends. (It didn't matter that Carl was five times older than Archibald and nearly six times larger.) Clementine was also aware that Carl's size made it difficult for him to leave the store where he lived. "All right Arch, you may go," she relented. "But take a flashlight. You'll need one in these conditions."

"Not me," Archibald said as he disappeared through an opaque curtain of fog. "I've got instincts."

Using his bare feet as sensors, Archibald followed the graveled driveway to the front gate, which he bumped into before climbing and proceeding up the muddied lane toward Route 628. Normally when Archibald went to Aylor's Store, he took the shortcut through the woods, but on this inclement day he prudently chose to follow the hardtop. The concept of prudence was relatively new to his character. In years past he would have charged headlong into a vast thicket at night. Not anymore. Now that he was nine, he was wiser than before— much shrewder about respecting the benefits of caution.

Thanks in part to luck, but mostly to a detailed knowledge of his surroundings, Archibald eventually found the porch at Aylor's Store, bounded up the steps and crossed to the front window, then cleared a circle of dew from the glass and peered inside. The lights were on, but he saw no one stirring about. He tried the door. It was unlocked.

As Archibald entered the store, he heard a low-pitched rumble coming from the rear of the building. It made him stop and smile. It was Carl, snoring. Only Carl could make that noise. The sound always reminded Archibald of thunder in a padded box.

Archibald hurried to the back of the store and hopped onto a flour barrel near Carl's feet. Carl's head was tilted backward, and Archibald could see directly into the cavernous chambers of his hairy snout. Intrigued, Archibald stared into the nasal abyss for approximately ten minutes while considering whether to awaken his big friend or not.

In the end Archibald decided to let Carl sleep. He hopped from the barrel and lifted his marble pouch off a nearby hook. From it he withdrew his favorite yellow shooting taw. Then he grabbed a roll of tape from behind the counter and carefully adhered his prize shooter to the boot-tip of Carl's right foot. The yellow marble was his calling card. When Carl awoke from his nap, he would know that Archibald had been in to see him.

The thick, dreamlike fog still hugged the land as Archibald left the store. He paused to pee in the parking lot, then headed east toward where Route 628 and the old Campbell's Creek Road connected with Route 631. The forked juncture was about a hundred yards from the store. Archibald planned to turn left at the fork and follow the old road to the Hillacre estate. He figured that after coming this far, he might as well pop by and see what Leopold and his great-aunt Emma were up to.

The summer before, Leopold and Emma had been wed in the Dithers' apple orchard at sunset on a new moon. A first for both, they had married for love and because they recognized that they complemented each other like pieces in a jigsaw puzzle. Leopold was a homegrown philosopher with a penchant for metaphysics, while Emma was a worldly individualist with a passion for psychospiritual investigations.

As Archibald plodded down the long hill toward the little bridge near Weeping Willow Swamp, Leopold Hillacre was reposing in his house atop a second hill on the far side of the bridge. To be more specific, Leopold was sitting in a swivel chair in the west wing of the house. The wing was basically one giant room with stained-glass windows and a twenty-two-foot cathedral ceiling. A black-marble fireplace was built into the north wall of the room, which was better known as the Inner Sanctum. On this vaporous morning, as Archibald approached the house, the remnants of a small fire still warmed the marble hearth. Leopold had not lit the fire for heat, but rather to fight the invasive moisture that was assaulting his books and precious manuscripts.

At seventy-five years of age, Leopold was a remarkably vital man. Although most of his hair had long ago parted company with his head, the brain inside his skull had never dulled. By any measure he was an original. As Jimmy Aylor, who owned the store and served as the county's unofficial pundit, once said, "Leopold Hillacre is so different from the rest of us, he's never even caught a common cold."

Leopold's bony hands were clasped around the nape of his neck, and his spindly legs were resting on the large oval worktable that dominated the Inner Sanctum. Cluttered around his feet in dog-eared stacks of yellowing paper was the unorganized body of the book that Leopold had been writing for the last fifty years. It was his magnum opus. He called it *The Comprehensive Guide*. So far he had generated over a thousand pages of handwritten text. Not a word of it was borrowed. It was highly original stuff.

Leopold was normally a cheerful, optimistic individual, but today his outlook was grim. Although the weather had something to do with his forbidding disposition, it was less of an influence than the cloud of personal doubts that had begun to form around him. Six weeks before (for reasons which he had now forgotten), he had convinced himself that *The Comprehensive Guide* was nearly ready for public consumption, and he had asked his new wife to query some of her publishing contacts in New York. Emma Bean had done so, and in the weeks following, Leopold had received letters from four publishing houses and two literary agencies. All were eager to consider the material. Of course, the prompt and positive responses were due largely to Emma Bean's reputation. In the previous decade, writing under a pseudonym, she had published several successful books on parapsychology and had written the forewords for two best-selling spy novels.

Most unpublished writers in Leopold's position would have been delighted by the response, yet he was far from pleased. In fact, he was beginning to wish he'd never opened his big mouth in the first place. The more he thought about sending the book out, the more he worried about the validity of certain passages, which led him to question entire chapters, which led him to doubt the fundamental merit of his life's work. And so on . . . until the cloud gathering around him was nearly as dense as the fog that enshrouded Willow County.

As Leopold ruminated, Emma sat at a table in the kitchen studying a drawing of her latest invention. The drawing had

taken two months to produce. Now, finally, Emma was satisfied with the design. She was in the act of signing her name on
the paper when she was startled by a knock at the door. Before
she could rise to see who was calling, Archibald barged into
the kitchen. "Wow. I made it," he said with evident relief. "It's
as thick as a thousand ghosts out there."

"Archibald." Emma said the name weakly.

Archibald bowed. Then his eye caught the drawing on the
table and he inquired, "Whatcha doing?"

"Working."

"Oh," said Archibald, his curiosity drawing him forward.

Emma leaned over the table and hid the drawing under an
elbow. "This is a private project."

Archibald stopped in his tracks and scrunched his face in
thought. Soon, though, his eyebrows arced upward and a grin
spread over his face. "Come on, Aunt Emma, let me see. I bet
you're just being modest."

Emma Bean snorted with amusement. She knew, of course,
that Archibald was trying to charm her into letting him look at
the drawing. Still, she admired people with curiosity and she
was impressed by his style. (He reminded her of a midget
swashbuckler she'd once met in Tunisia.) "Go ahead," she said,
sitting back and gesturing at the drawing. "Take a look."

Archibald approached the table and studied the drawing
with the ponderous air of a structural engineer inspecting
blueprints for a power plant. He nodded, tapped the paper
with a finger, and mumbled, "That's excellent. But what is it?"

Emma weighed Archibald with a long look before answering,
"That's a design for an Astral Projector."

Archibald grimaced, as though disappointed with himself.
"I should have known. That's what I thought it was at first."

At this moment Leopold wandered into the kitchen and

greeted the unexpected visitor with a lazy wave. "You must have swum through the fog to get here."

"Just followed my toes," Archibald said ingenuously.

Leopold pointed his nose at the drawing on the table. "I see you're assisting Emma with her latest project."

"Yes," Archibald replied with a straight face. "We're working on a Pastoral Ejector."

Leopold erupted with laughter and was soon quaking so violently he fell against a cabinet for support.

Archibald frowned and turned to Emma Bean. "What's wrong with him?"

Emma hurried to Leopold's aid. She took his arm, guided him to a chair, and patted his back until he resumed a regular breathing pattern. Then she answered Archibald, "Leopold has always been vulnerable to words. I believe he was tickled by your spoonerism."

Archibald's frown became an angry scowl. He did not enjoy being left out on a joke. "I'm glad he's tickled, but what is a spoonerism?"

Emma smiled patiently and replied, "A spoonerism is when someone transposes the initial sounds in a word combination. This is a drawing for an Astral Projector. Not a Pastoral Ejector."

"Excuse me," Archibald said. "I didn't know there was a difference."

Leopold's owlish eyes bulged in their sockets and his hands began to tremble. Then he gasped for air and doubled over with renewed hysterics.

Chapter Two

It was almost noon. Henry Dither stood in the parlor of his home gazing absentmindedly through the window. Behind him, in her crib, his youngest daughter Angeline was singing her latest musical composition. Angeline was eighteen months old. Henry was convinced that she was a prodigy. She had curly dark hair and big brown eyes.

The parlor window was in the rear of the house, facing west. Usually when Henry gazed from this window he saw apple trees lining the ridge. Today all he saw was a pearl-gray wall of fog pressing against the windowpane.

Angeline hit a high note, held it in a trill, then cooed a couple of counterpoint oohs and aahs. Henry, lost in abstraction, turned and watched her for a moment. A moment later he shuffled out of the parlor.

Holly was sewing mirrored sequins on her show jacket

when Henry wandered into the kitchen. "Hi, Pop," she chirped merrily, doing a double take as she noticed the troubled look on his face. "Hey, Mom, you better grab a look at Dad. Something's wrong. He might be wibberniffled again."

Holly's twelve-year-old sister Matilda lifted her nose from the book she was reading and said, "Don't be so daft, Holly. The weather is disrupting his bio-rhythms. He's not wibberniffled."

Holly, who was fourteen, groaned and returned to her sewing. Matilda snickered and flipped the page. She was an avid reader with an expansive vocabulary and she enjoyed using elaborate words such as *bio-rhythms.*

Clementine (for whom Henry had invented the word *wibberniffled*, which means lost in a dream with the one you love) turned from the kitchen window and eyed her husband with a concerned smile. She knew it was hard for him to linger idly in the house for a whole day, much less four. It was clear to her that he needed something to do. "Henry, honey, do me a favor?" she said softly.

"Sure. Glad to. What?"

"Go check on Emmet. He's been in the barn since breakfast."

"On my way." He sounded grateful. As he left the kitchen, he bent and kissed the top of Holly's head. "Don't mind Matilda. I'm wibberniffled every time I see my girls."

Immediately upon opening and stepping through the barn door, Henry stumbled and threw his hands up to shield his eyes. Someone had aimed a cluster of floodlights at the entrance. He guessed who that someone was even before his pupils adjusted and he could see Emmet. Sure enough, as his field of vision returned, he saw his thirteen-year-old son standing in a pool of brightness. Squatting at Emmet's side was his boon companion, an eleven-pound rhesus monkey named Senator.

Emmet wore a folded red bandana across his forehead. In his right hand he held a wooden hoop about the size of a trash-can lid. Already an accomplished juggler, Emmet had recently decided to be a professional vaudevillian when he grew up and was working diligently to develop the necessary skills. The fact that vaudeville had died thirty years earlier did not discourage him in the least. When Emmet saw Henry at the door, he cried excitedly, "Hey, Dad, watch. I want to show you something."

"I'm watching."

Emmet flashed a hand signal at Senator before yanking the headband down over his eyes. As his sidekick darted across the barn floor toward a chalk mark, Emmet rotated three times. By now Senator had sprung onto his front paws and stuck his tail straight up in the air. "Ready, Dad? Are you watching?"

"Go ahead, son."

Emmet flicked the hoop horizontally toward his unseen target. It whooshed through the air before striking the monkey smack in the middle of his upside-down chest. Senator squealed, dropped to his feet, and picked up the hoop.

Holly's pony Dan had been watching the show from his stall. He threw back his head and neighed.

"How'd I do?" Emmet asked as he reached for the blindfold.

"Keep practicing, son," Henry muttered. "You'll get there."

Senator, unable to express his feelings in words, hurled the hoop toward the rafters. At the zenith of its arc, the wooden ring caught on a peg and dangled.

At twenty minutes to two on Wednesday, after serving the lunch she had prepared for Archibald, Emma opened the kitchen door and peered searchingly at the sky. She had sensed a subtle shift in the atmosphere—a minute change in the density of light. And it wasn't wishful thinking. She was just in time to watch as a cylindrical shaft of sunlight burned a hole in the miasmic ceiling over Weeping Willow Swamp. Pent-up light fell earthward, bounced off the bog and flooded into the surrounding thickets. Emma cheered. The fog was lifting, which meant that Archibald would be going soon. Having finished the design for her Astral Projector, she wanted to contemplate its significance in solitude.

Henry was also watching as the sun tore through the fog. To him it seemed as as if he was witnessing a minor miracle. One moment the world was hidden, and the next moment it was revealed in all its green splendor. Hallelujah. Droplets of dew on the grass sparkled like a harvest of diamonds.

About a half hour after the sun reasserted its dominance over a blue sky, Flea Jenfries and Warren Robinson arrived at Dither Farm in Flea's station wagon. Warren, who first visited the county two years before with Emma Bean, had been adopted by Flea. He was fourteen. Originally the Dithers had planned to adopt him, but when Flea heard of their intentions she argued that Clementine and Henry already had plenty of kids and that she deserved to have at least one. Clementine had wisely deferred the decision to Warren, who at the time had a mad crush on Holly. After taking all things into consideration, he chose to live with Flea.

Clementine greeted Flea in the yard, directed Warren to the tree fort where Emmet and Senator had gone after the sun came out, then ushered her guest to the front porch. The two women had arrangements to make. Holly had been hired to ride in the Wild West show at Queen's Playland that summer, and Flea had offered to go along as her chaperon. Holly was due to begin rehearsals at the amusement park in ten days. She and Flea would be housed in a staff apartment on the grounds. Holly's pony Dan would reside in a modern, climate-controlled barn. Although the details were not yet confirmed, the plan was for Flea to stay with Holly until the end of July; then either Millie Ross or Bellamonte Smoot would assume Flea's duties in August.

"I spoke with Garland," Flea said after she and Clementine were settled. "He's fixed the hitch on his trailer and said he'd be glad to haul Dan on the twenty-first."

"That's sweet of Garland," noted Clementine. "Before you go, I'll give you some money for expenses."

"No need for that," Flea protested. "Our lodging and meals are free, and you'll be keeping Warren while I'm away."

"Nonsense," Clementine countered. "I'm giving you a hundred dollars for gas and incidentals. It'll come out of Holly's first check."

Under ordinary circumstances Flea would never have accepted money from Clementine; but since Holly would be earning the astounding sum of three hundred dollars a week, Flea decided to make an exception. She would give fifty to Garland for his troubles and save the rest for emergencies.

Having settled that issue, Clementine allowed her mind to drift to other matters: Specifically, she was curious about Flea's love life. It was common knowledge in Willow County that Garland Barlow and Flea had developed romantic feelings for each other, but Clementine wanted details. Had Flea and Garland discussed prospects for a future? Clementine began tentatively. "I, ah . . . was just wondering, how is Garland?

Will he stay the night after he drives you and Holly and Dan to Queen's Playland?"

Flea turned as pink as a peony. "He might . . . if he's tired, and if there's a sofa bed in the apartment."

"Oh, I'm sure they'll have a sofa bed," Clementine said with alacrity.

"They must," Flea agreed nervously. "I'm sure they must."

The two friends were saved from further embarrassment by Holly's appearance on the porch. She was carrying Angeline, whom she handed to Clementine. "You said if I watched her you'd change her when she was ready," Holly informed her mother, wrinkling her nose and adding, "I believe she's past ready."

"So," Flea said to Holly. "Are you getting excited yet?"

"Me, excited?" Holly replied jokingly. "I'm as calm as a kitten at a dog show."

Emmet, Warren, and Senator were on the backside of the farm, relaxing in the tree fort that Senator called home. They passed a bag of peanuts back and forth, casually tossing the shucked shells into the leafy green world below.

For the past half hour Emmet had been raving about the merits of vaudeville. He was trying to convince Warren to join his act. "I'm telling you, variety entertainment is the wave of the future."

Warren shrugged, convinced of nothing.

"Let Holly have the big top," Emmet said with a dismissive grunt. "I'm heading for the stage. And, Warren, if you were smart, you'd be right behind me."

Warren made no reply. He did not even bother to shrug.

"It's the good life!" Emmet said passionately. "Acrobatics.

Miming. Juggling. Song and dance. Physical comedy. You get to travel all the time and you never have to work in the mornings."

Warren took the peanut bag from Senator and looked askance at Emmet. "Did it ever occur to you that I'm not the type for going on stage . . . that maybe I'm just not interested?"

"What? Not interested in getting rich?"

Warren frowned. "Getting rich wouldn't hurt . . . if that's what happened. It seems rather unlikely to me."

Emmet shook his head in disbelief. "I don't understand you, Warren. You should be jumping at the chance to join my act."

Warren shucked and ate a peanut, handed the bag back to Senator, and turned to face Emmet. "Want to know what I think?"

"Sure."

"Well, to begin with, you are a pretty good juggler. I'll admit that. But otherwise I think you're just in this because of Contessa Cunningham. You never even thought about vaudeville until she told you she wanted to train her pet pig to dance."

Emmet gave Warren a stinging look. He leaned back on his elbows, sulked for a moment, then finally conceded, "You're right. Contessa gave me the idea."

"I thought so."

"That doesn't mean it's a bad idea. In fact, it just proves that all the really pretty girls are drawn to the stage."

Suddenly—for no evident reason—Senator jumped to his feet, squealed, and leaped from the tree fort.

Emmet was not amused. "Silly creature."

Warren leaned forward and watched as Senator caught

ahold of a branch and suspended himself by his tail. "That monkey is going to be a big star one day."

"I know," said Emmet. "That's why I signed him to an exclusive contract. Perhaps when we're famous, we'll let you visit us backstage."

"You don't give up, do you?" said Warren.

"No," Emmet replied flatly. "Not when my own best friend doesn't know what's good for him."

Chapter Three

Now that Emma Bean's design for the Astral Projector was complete, she began making arrangements to produce the contraption. The first thing she needed was the components, and for them she paid a call on the only welder she knew, Garland Barlow. After hearing her odd request, Garland told Emma, "I'll have to order the brass rods. That could take a week or so."

"How long, total, do you think?" asked Emma. She was eager to get started.

"Let's see. A day to make the couplings and weld the hooks. Another day for Acorn and Bart to polish the fittings and coil the wire. If the parts come on time and all goes well, I might be done ten days from now."

Emma calculated swiftly. "That's the weekend after next. Can you deliver?"

Garland nodded. "Sure. But if I'm not done by then, you'll have to wait until the following week. I'm hauling Holly Dither's pony to Queen's Playland on the twenty-first. I might not return until Monday."

"Give my love to Flea," Emma said with a wink.

Garland blushed and looked away. "So . . . mind telling me what you intend to do with seventy-two feet of three-inch brass rods and ninety-nine feet of coiled copper wire?"

"Sorry, that's confidential information," Emma said politely yet firmly.

Garland shrugged. He knew enough about Emma to guess that she was preparing for an experiment, yet he could not imagine what it might be. He was particularly intrigued by her instructions that the wire be twisted into double helixes.

"Present a bill when you deliver the stuff. I'll pay cash."

Garland nodded. A job was a job. He was glad for the income.

Before leaving on her bicycle, Emma paused to chat with Acorn and Bart. They were brothers and they lived in the converted chicken coop behind Garland's shop. They had moved there after standing trial with their uncle for kidnapping Archibald Dither. The uncle was a cruel and nefarious fellow named Crowley Hogget. Garland had saved the boys from incarceration by speaking to the judge on their behalf. He argued that Crowley had bullied his nephews into committing the crime. The judge had agreed and released the two brothers into Garland's care. Technically they were on probation. "Howdy, fellows," Emma said cheerfully.

"Hello, Mrs. Hillacre," Acorn responded. He was more social than his awkward brother, and smarter, too.

"So, how goes the honest life?" asked Emma.

"Not too bad," allowed Acorn. "The food is regular and we're both saving a little money."

Bart, a chronic question-asker, leaned over and whispered to Acorn, "Does she know about our education?"

Acorn acknowledged Bart with a look and explained to Emma, "He was reminding me about the lessons Millie Ross is giving us. She comes once a week. She's teaching us to read and write and to understand theories about some big stuff you can't see."

Emma laughed. "Be careful with those theories. People have gone over the edge thinking about big stuff."

Acorn's eye widened, and he shuddered. The edge was a concept that he fearfully respected.

As Emma pedaled from the property, Bart tapped Acorn on the shoulder. "Did you forget that we're learning arithmetic, too?"

"Naw. I just didn't tell her. That's all."

Anyone who has ever visited Willow County knows the place is so flush with time its residents always have plenty to spare. Rarely do Willowites grow anxious about clocks or calendars. Why should they? That would be like Bedouins worrying about the supply of sand. Yet as Holly Dither anticipated making her debut in the Wild West show at Queen's Playland, it seemed that the desert stretched endlessly before her and she might die of thirst before reaching the oasis in the distance.

Finally, though, like a camel with a one-track mind, Holly made it to the well. When she awoke at dawn on the third Sunday in June, she sat up in bed and hollered, "Whoop-de-do! Yip, yip, yippity-yo!"

"Please," Matilda groaned. "I'm trying to sleep."

"Just practicing my cowgirl calls," Holly explained.

"Go practice with the cows. This is a bedroom. It was designed for sleeping."

"Don't be so grouchy," Holly huffed. "Today I leave to entertain the masses. You'll have the bedroom all to yourself for the rest of the summer. The least you can do is let me practice my calls."

Matilda considered telling Holly to go suck a goose egg. Instead she rolled onto her stomach and pulled the covers over her head. As everyone with a sibling knows, sometimes it is best not to argue.

Holly dressed and went down the stairs to the kitchen. It was a quarter to six as she put a kettle on the stove for tea. Although she had no way of knowing it, Holly was not the only person in her end of Willow County who was wide awake at that moment. Less than a mile east of the farm, Carl Plummers was sitting upright on the edge of a king-sized bed in his cramped room behind the store. There was a look of astonished fright in his eyes, and his forehead was covered in sweat. Carl had been awoken by a disturbing dream.

Carl went to his dresser, opened a drawer, and took out a tattered envelope containing an old black-and-white photograph. He removed the picture, returned to his bed, and sat down to look at the image. It was Carl's most-prized possession. The picture had been taken almost forty years before. It was the only tangible reminder Carl owned of his twin sister, Stella.

As the picture revealed, Stella had been a beautiful child, with high cheekbones and long, flowing hair. There was a sharp look in her eyes and a hint of mischievous humor in her smile. A boy stood by her side. He appeared frightened by the camera and had turned to Stella for reassurance. It was Carl. He and his sister were standing on the steps of the orphanage where they had lived since infancy.

Carl's chubby hands trembled and his eyes blurred with tears as he studied the old picture. One week after he and his sister had celebrated their eleventh birthday, Stella caught pneumonia. She died three days later. The loss for Carl had been greater than the sum value of the world.

And now, odd as it may seem, Carl's grief welled up inside him with all the sorrowful pain of his original bereavement. Intermittently throughout his adolescent and adult life Carl had received visits from Stella in his dreams. Once every month or so, sometimes more, she would appear at his side and remind him that he was loved. It was Carl's big secret. His knowledge that Stella still existed and cared for him had carried Carl through the many troubled phases of his life.

But last night Stella had come to warn him that her visits might soon cease forever. Her words echoed sadly in his head: "Carl, it's me. Listen closely. I want you to keep the vow we made together. I'm growing weaker and I don't know if I will have the strength to return. Please, remember your promise to me."

Carl had awoken and called, "Stella. Don't go."

"Remember," Stella whispered before vanishing into the void.

"What?" Carl cried, although he could feel that Stella had already gone.

For the life of him, Carl struggled to remember making a vow to Stella. But he could not remember, and as the pastel light of dawn brushed his bedroom window, he stared at the photograph and pleaded, "Please, Stella, don't go. Come back and tell me what the promise was. I can't remember."

A ray of sunlight suddenly poked through the dingy curtains and struck Carl's face. For an instant he sensed a shimmering presence in the room above him. He looked hopefully upward. A tiny light blinked, as if a firefly was in the room. Then there was nothing . . . except for the chilling feeling that someone had kissed the top of his head.

Early that afternoon, as many of the good people in Willow County were returning home from church, Archibald and Matilda stood at the Hillacres' kitchen door, waiting for someone to reply to their knocks. With them was Matilda's hound dog, Goosebumps. He had one blue eye and one green one. Wherever Matilda went, he liked to follow. Matilda was at the door because she wanted to speak with Leopold about a section of *The Comprehensive Guide* she'd read the night before. Archibald was there to see if the parts for Emma Bean's Astral Projector had arrived. He planned to offer his assistance in building the contraption.

Emma answered after the tenth knock. "Did you get the parts for your thingamajig?" Archibald asked before Emma could speak.

Emma cleared her throat to answer, but then Matilda inquired, "Is Leopold in the Inner Sanctum?"

"No, the parts haven't arrived," Emma said quickly to Archibald, then told Matilda, "Leopold is in the cupola. He didn't sleep very well last night. Neither did I."

"I slept like a log," Archibald noted cheerfully. "So, we have only a couple of hours to kill before we have to go home and say good-bye to Holly. She leaves today for Queen's Playland. Too bad about the parts. I came to help you."

Emma heaved a rueful sigh. "Thanks for the offer, but I won't be needing any help."

"No? Why not?"

"Because . . . it's a delicate project."

"I'm good with delicate," Archibald countered. "Angeline is delicate, and Mom lets me hold her."

Emma rolled her eyes. She was preparing to answer Archibald when Matilda said, "Excuse me," and stepped past her into the kitchen. She turned at the foot of the steps leading up to the cupola and told Goosebumps to wait.

Goosebumps gave Matilda a disappointed look, then flopped on the floor like a good dog.

Archibald backed Emma into the kitchen, where they continued their debate about whether or not she would be needing an assistant.

Leopold was standing on the north side of the cupola, gazing out over the expanse of Weeping Willow Swamp, when Matilda appeared. He made no sign of noticing her. She waited for several minutes before finally coughing to announce herself. He did not turn; yet after an extended pause he moaned despairingly, "Jupiter save me."

Matilda had no idea what he was talking about. "From what?"

"From my miserable self," Leopold answered gravely. "I've just realized what a fool I've been."

"You? A fool? No way," Matilda said incredulously. She knew no one wiser than Leopold.

Leopold turned slowly from the window. His face was ashen and he spoke with dark seriousness. "Yes, Matilda, I'm a fool. It's not something I'm proud of, but it's true."

Matilda was shocked. "Wha . . . what are you talking about? Why do you say that?"

Leopold smiled bitterly and explained, "I've decided against publishing *The Comprehensive Guide*. The writing is a wash. It's worthless. It stinks."

Matilda could hardly believe her ears. "Leopold, the *Guide* is brilliant."

"My Matilda . . . so supportive. But I know when I'm beat. My book is an ugly creature." Leopold turned wearily back to the window and mused aloud, "Fifty years down the drain. The whole time I believed I was worthy of Socrates, of Spinoza, of Swami Vivekananda . . . but no! I was laboring under an illusion."

It was clear to Matilda that Leopold was having a mental crisis, and she sensed that she should say something soothing. But what? How could she tell the smartest man she knew that he was not thinking clearly? What could she say? Then Matilda recalled a passage in Leopold's book that she had read the night before, and she decided to address him in his own words. " 'There are three dimensions to every idea: the inside, the outside, and the surface. A person seeing the surface can name the idea, yet not know its inner nature. A person seeing the outside can know its inner nature, but never grasp its higher purpose. Only someone who penetrates the inside of an idea can perceive its true value.' "

When Leopold turned and sank down on the bench below the window, a bit of color had returned to his face. Unfortunately, it was the blush of embarrassment. "Philosophical frippery. Written by a deluded intellectual with nothing to say."

"Your book isn't frippery," Matilda replied with heated conviction. "In fact, it deals squarely with those elusive truths you admire so much. I don't know how or when it happened, but I think you've gotten stuck on the surface of a bad idea."

Leopold grimaced at Matilda and shook his head.

Matilda was encouraged. Leopold's expression was grim, yet behind his bluer-than-blue eyes she saw an open mind. He wasn't ready to agree with her, yet he was willing to listen. "I'm no philosopher," she began gently. "But I am your friend, and that entitles me to speak my mind. Maybe I don't understand every idea you've put in *The Comprehensive Guide*, but I've read the book and it caused me to think of things I'd never considered before. That makes it important. It'd be a shame to throw it out because of a few flaws that can be fixed." Matilda paused and studied the tired look on Leopold's face. It inspired her to suggest, "I think you should take a vacation before making any drastic decisions."

Leopold blinked, a flicker of interest appearing in his defeated eyes. "A vacation?"

Matilda nodded. "You've been working too hard. Go somewhere for a week or two and forget all about *The Comprehensive Guide*."

Leopold did not dismiss the suggestion outright, nor did he give any sign of endorsing it.

"I quote you again," said Matilda. " 'Inspiration is a coy woman. If you court her too hard, she ignores you. Yet when you wander from her chamber, she whispers your name.' "

Leopold hemmed thoughtfully and rubbed his chin. "Wander from her chamber . . . yes . . . a vacation. But where would I go?"

Chapter Four

Shortly after noon on Sunday, about twenty minutes after Archibald, Matilda, and Goosebumps departed for home, Garland arrived at the Hillacre estate with the parts for Emma Bean's experiment. When Emma went to greet Garland, he stuck his head out the truck window and called, "Hello, Emma. I'm in a hurry. Where do you want this stuff?"

Emma pointed to the carriage house, where she planned to work on her invention. "By the door is fine. What do I owe you?"

"Two hundred bucks," Garland replied, shifting his truck into reverse and backing up to the old wooden structure. Emma returned just as Garland pulled the last rod off the truck and set it on the ground. She handed him a wad of bills, which he stuffed in a hip pocket without bothering to count.

"I put an extra twenty in there for delivery," said Emma.

"Thanks," Garland said as he moved to get back in his truck. "So what's the big rush?"

Garland started his engine and leaned out the window. "Gotta shower, fetch Flea and Warren, drive to Dither Farm to pick up Holly and her pony Dan, then drive to Queen's Playland."

Matilda was in the yard when Garland, Flea, and Warren arrived at Dither Farm. "Holly isn't ready to go yet," Matilda said with a laugh. "Poor girl. She only had two months to prepare. Mom is upstairs with her now, helping her pack."

Warren leaped from the back of the truck to join Emmet and Senator on the fence. Flea paused to chat with Matilda for a moment, then went upstairs to confabulate with Clementine and Holly. Garland wandered into the parlor, where he found Archibald and Henry being serenaded by Angeline. Henry motioned for Garland to join him on the couch and whispered, "Prepare to hear the voice of an angel." Garland gave Henry a skeptical look and sat back to listen. A moment later his mouth was agape in awe.

Finally, at three o'clock, Holly led Dan from the barn to the trailer behind Garland's truck. Clementine and Henry stood hand in hand in the driveway, watching as Garland helped Holly adjust the loading ramp. Angeline was asleep in a stroller next to Clementine. Matilda, Emmet, Warren, Archibald, and Senator sat on the fence. Flea waited in the cab of the truck.

"There she goes, off to make her fortune," Henry mumbled to Clementine. "Seems like yesterday she was a baby."

"And look at her now," Clementine observed wryly. "She's

wearing cowboy boots and tight white jeans . . . going away without a doubt in her head."

"She always was headstrong," Henry noted.

"You mean ambitious, don't you?" Clementine replied. "Don't forget, Holly has wanted to be famous since she could walk."

"True," Henry agreed. "Last night I heard her telling Emmet that all the really big stars start shining early in life."

"That's our Holly . . . modest to the bone."

After Dan was settled, Garland slid the ramp into its carrying bin and joined Flea in the cab of the truck while Holly bid her adieus. Holly began with Matilda. "Enjoy the room, sis. You can use my closet, but don't touch anything in my dresser."

"Don't worry," said Matilda. "Everything will be just where you left it when you get back. So have a good time."

"Thanks. You take care. I'll see you when you visit."

"Yep," said Matilda, reaching to shake her sister's hand.

Holly turned next to Emmet. "See ya, brother. Keep practicing those routines. Maybe one day when you're ready, I'll drop your name to a booking agent."

"Gee, thanks," Emmet said with a mock smile. "Good luck with your job. I hope you stay out of trouble."

"Me? Trouble?" Holly laughed before moving down the fence to Warren. He dropped to the ground and looked shyly into Holly's eyes. There were certain matters of the heart he had wished to discuss with Holly before she went away, yet for various reasons he'd not had the chance to speak his mind. And now, with everyone watching, he felt constrained. So he extended a hand and said simply, "Good-bye, Holly. I'll miss you."

"Isn't that sweet," Holly chirped, ignoring the proffered hand and stepping forward to kiss Warren's cheek. Then, much to his chagrin, she added loudly enough for all to hear, "Unless one of my costars sweeps me off my feet, I'll miss you, too."

Warren winced with embarrassment, thankful for the distraction as Archibald erupted with laughter and fell from the fence. He lay on his back and addressed his older sister with exaggerated sincerity, "I love you, Holly. Please don't change just because you're a big shot now."

Holly smirked and put her hands on her hips. "Don't worry, I won't, but I will say a prayer for you."

"Oh, bless your sweet soul," Archibald cackled before rolling into the ditch beside him.

Holly shook her head and turned to Henry, who embraced her in a bear hug and declared, "Holly, you're a credit to the Dither name. I want you to show those folks at Queen's Playland what we're made of here in Willow County."

"That's my plan, Dad."

Henry grinned. "Behave yourself and remember to call if you feel lonely."

"Got it," said Holly. She withdrew from Henry's embrace and bent to kiss the sleeping Angeline. When she rose, Clementine took her arm and led her slowly toward the cab of the truck. Both daughter and mother had big brown eyes, luxuriant dark hair, and curvaceous figures. Although Holly's physique wasn't quite as developed as Clementine's, it was noticeably feminine and was the source of some concern for Clementine. To her it seemed as if Holly had become a woman overnight. "Remember all the things I told you," Clementine instructed. "You're growing up fast, but you've got a long way to go before you're a grown-up. Understand?"

"Yes, Mom," Holly replied impatiently. Clementine had given her a long lecture while they were packing.

"And don't forget," Clementine continued. "Flea's the boss. Whatever she says goes. No arguments."

"Okay, okay."

Clementine sighed and hugged Holly good-bye. "We'll see you in a couple of weeks, then. I love you."

Holly responded warmly to the hug and kissed her mother lightly on the cheek. "Please, don't have a cow fretting about me. I know the difference between right and wrong."

"Of course you do," Clementine agreed. "You're a Dither."

As Garland drove away from Dither Farm at three thirty that afternoon, Leopold Hillacre was still sitting in the cupola where Matilda had left him. Her suggestion that he take a vacation had appealed to Leopold's imagination, and within ten minutes of her departure he had decided upon a visit to the seaside. It was the question of which seaside that had kept him thinking. During the past few hours he'd traveled mentally around the world. Hawaii . . . Polynesia . . . the coast of India . . . a Caribbean island. Leopold was searching for the perfect beach where he might spend an idle week or month or whatever. As he reasoned: "I'm seventy-five years old. I can do whatever tickles my fancy."

Archibald headed to Aylor's Store after Holly's send-off. In a break with the normal rhythm of things, he had not spoken to Carl for nearly a week. It wasn't Archibald's fault; on each of his last three visits, Carl had been napping.

Today Carl was awake when Archibald appeared in the back of the store, yet it was apparent at a glance that something was wrong with the big fellow. He was slumped down in his seat and his eyes were hooded with dark lines. "Are you all right?" Archibald asked.

Carl acknowledged his visitor with a wrinkled brow, but he did not say a word.

"You look like you've seen a ghost."

Carl moaned.

Archibald was alarmed. He'd seen Carl displeased with things before, he'd even seen him get mad temporarily, but this was the first time he'd glimpsed such pain and sorrow in the man. Archibald fidgeted nervously. It seemed as if Carl was about to start crying. "Listen, pal," Archibald said tentatively. "I know something is wrong. Can I help?"

Carl frowned gloomily and crossed his chubby arms.

"Want to talk about it?"

"No," Carl said in a low, wobbly voice. "Not today."

Archibald's alarm turned to fright. The situation was worse than he'd first realized. "Okay. That's okay," he said softly. "I'll come back tomorrow. Maybe you'll feel like talking then."

"Maybe," Carl mumbled sadly.

Advertised as "Royal fun for all ages," Queen's Playland sported a roller coaster, a Ferris wheel, a water slide, a house of mirrors, an air tunnel, and a bullet swing. The park also contained a saltwater lagoon, a ten-story model of the Eiffel Tower, and a restaurant-shopping complex. As an added attraction throughout July and August, Queen's Playland offered a theatrical extravaganza called the Wild West show.

To drive by truck with a trailer in tow it took just over two hours to get from Dither Farm to Queen's Playland. Garland pulled up to the colonnaded entrance at a quarter past five and was greeted by a uniformed attendant. The man looked at Holly's papers, made a radio call, then directed Garland toward the air-conditioned barn where Dan would be housed. "After you get the pony settled, one of the Glee Guides will show you to your apartment."

"Glee Guides?" asked Garland.

"Public-relations personnel. You can't miss them. Just look for a smiling teenager wearing a green jacket."

Garland nodded and prepared to pull forward. The attendant halted him with a gesture. "I almost forgot. There's a reception dinner tonight for all Wild West performers and their chaperons. It starts at seven thirty. Ask a Glee Guide for directions to the Paradise Club."

"The Paradise Club!" Holly trilled as the truck lurched forward. "What am I going to wear?"

Later that evening, as Holly, Flea, and Garland were relaxing in the apartment at Queen's Playland, Leopold Hillacre was telling Emma Bean about his vacation plans. The longer Emma listened to her excited husband, the more forbidding her frown became. When he noticed her unhappiness, he paused to let her speak. She did so in a soft yet authoritative manner. "Like it or not, Leopold, you are my husband now, and I don't believe I want you trotting off to some distant patch of sand where women of questionable morals loll around all day in French bikinis."

Leopold was taken aback. "I, ah . . . I wasn't thinking of a social escape. My intentions are to get some rest. Maybe build a few castles in the sand."

Emma shook her head doubtfully. "If you do go anywhere— just supposing—it will not be for an indefinite period of time."

"Of course not," Leopold agreed. "I was just being symbolic when I said the word *month*. You know . . . poetic."

"I understand," Emma replied with a thin smile. "You'll go for a week and then you'll come home."

Leopold grimaced. He'd been a bachelor for seventy-four years, and it was not easy for him to suddenly obey the wishes of someone else—even if that someone was the woman he loved. Still, he agreed: "A week should be sufficient."

A kind of victorious smile appeared on Emma's face. "I must confess, a dip in the sea sounds rather appealing right now. If it wasn't for my project, I'd come with you."

Leopold offered Emma a sympathetic look. "Too bad you can't come, Emma. It would've been nice. Maybe next time."

Emma knew Leopold was inwardly relieved, and that was fine with her. She believed it was good for couples to spend time apart periodically. And besides, Leopold really did need a break from his desk. "Next time," she said with one of her trademark snorts. "Now we just need to decide where you'll go."

Leopold nodded and waited. Knowing Emma Bean the way he did, he expected her to follow the remark with a suggestion.

She did. "I hear Virginia Beach is pleasant this time of year. No sense traveling farther than necessary."

Leopold acquiesced with a shrug. It wasn't Polynesia, but it was better than not going anywhere at all.

"Virginia Beach it is, then," Emma said pleasantly. "Glad you agree. Next time I'm near a phone, I'll see what I can do about arranging accommodations for you and Matilda."

"Excuse me?"

"Surely you don't intend to go alone?"

Leopold swallowed; he was in love with a dictator. For an instant he considered resisting Emma's wishes, but he was afraid if he argued she might impose additional restrictions. "Of course I'll want company," he said with forced cheer. "Matilda will make the best of companions."

Emma Bean rose up on her toes and kissed Leopold on the cheek. He was a good husband and she wanted him to know he was appreciated.

Holly could hardly believe her own good fortune. The waiting was over. She could stop fighting the minutes. Two or three more of them and she would stroll down Squire's Lane and enter the Paradise Club. She, a humble equestrienne from Willow County, would soon be dining in a room full of professional entertainers. She had chosen to wear a pleated white skirt and a red silk blouse for the momentous occasion.

Then the moment came and Holly pushed open the door to the Paradise Club. Flea and Garland, appropriately attired in their Sunday best, followed her down an elegant hallway and into a cavernous room filled with Holly's peers. The room was a marvel. A bluish light emanated from hundreds of starfish recessed in a stuccoed ceiling. The walls were adorned with murals of mermaids and shipwrecked sailors. There were palm trees in the corners and a thin layer of sand on the floor.

Holly felt like she had died and gone to the Academy Awards. Including chaperons, performers, and staff, roughly fifty people had gathered for dinner. While Garland gawked at the mermaids, Holly and Flea studied the crowd and noted that many of the female guests had a taste for modern fashion.

Soon a tall, muscular woman with short dark hair approached a podium in the center of the room. She wore gray slacks with a matching jacket. She introduced herself as Sally Swope, the director of the Wild West show. She was clearly a no-nonsense sort of person. "You are paid enter-tainers now and it's my job to see that you look like profes-sionals when we open the show in ten days. I'm good at my job. If you are good at yours, we'll get along swell. All new-comers will report to the south stadium at seven tomorrow morning. Those performers returning from last year, join us at nine. I advise everyone to eat a hearty breakfast. The first day is always the longest." Sally paused to inspect her audience, then announced before leaving the podium, "Tonight is for having fun. Performers will find place cards on the front tables. Chaperons sit in back."

Holly noticed that some of the other girls her age appeared as nervous as she felt inside, so she decided to distinguish her-self with composure. She drew a deep breath and nodded to Flea and Garland before sauntering confidently across the crowded room. Anyone studying her closely would've seen that she was overacting, yet there was so much stirring about, no one noticed. It was for the best, because as soon as Holly found her place card and saw the fellow in the chair next to her chair, she lost all pretense of self-possession. She thought she might faint when he turned toward her and said in a silky drawl, "If I may introduce myself, I'm Beaufort B. Beaumont."

Holly, too tongue-tied to speak, sank down and pointed at her place card.

Beaufort did not even glance at the card. "I know who you are, Holly Dither. Sally says you're going to be my costar this year."

Chapter Five

Since Warren would be staying with the Dithers until Flea returned from Queen's Playland, Archibald was booted out of the bedroom he shared with Emmet and sent to spend his nights on a cot in the pantry. Archibald was familiar with the arrangement. Although he complained to the authorities about the switch, he did so on principle, not because he actually minded sleeping in the pantry. The cot sagged and there was an odor of cleaning agents in the room, yet it was conveniently located for late-night raids on the kitchen and it provided him with easy egress through the back door.

He awoke at the crack of ten thirty on Monday morning. After stepping into his red shorts and pulling on a slightly soiled T-shirt, he ate the remains of a peanut-butter-and-jelly sandwich before leaving the house. He was on his way to see Carl.

When Archibald arrived at the store, Carl was napping, so he grabbed an *Incredible Romance* magazine off the rack and hopped onto the flour barrel. A few minutes later, engrossed in a story about a couple who'd gotten married and divorced three times, he heard the distinctive sound of his great-aunt's voice. "Hello, Jimmy," said Emma as she waltzed behind the counter and put a hand on the phone. "I'm making a toll-free call. Thanks."

"Go right ahead," acceded Jimmy. (He knew that Leopold had owned a phone once but had gotten rid of it two days later when an aluminum-siding salesman dared to disturb his afternoon nap.) It was fine with him if Emma made an occasional call, just as long as he was there to eavesdrop. Keeping up with Emma Bean was one of Jimmy's favorite pastimes.

Emma dialed an unlisted number in Washington, D.C., and waited until the phone at the National Security desk in the White House was answered. When it was, she said: "Good day, Simmons. E. Bean here. I need that favor you owe me." There was a pause; then Emma snorted and said, "Your memory must be leaking again. Don't you remember the film I made during our party in Winchester?" Emma listened, then said with a snicker, "I knew I could count on your cooperation. I need access to a safe house in Virginia Beach. For two, in early July. My husband and a guest." There was a long pause that Emma ended in a sharp tone: "Listen, you swine. Unless you want to be a popular film star, send a map and a key today. You have my address." Emma listened for a moment longer, laughed loudly, and hung up the phone.

Jimmy knew better than to meddle in Emma's business, and so he didn't ask her any questions as she started for the door. He did, however, eye her with a look of hungry curiosity.

Emma, aware of Jimmy's gaze, turned on her way out and said with a teasing wink, "Sometimes you have to hit people over the head for a favor."

Archibald caught up with his aunt as she was descending the porch steps. She did not break her stride and he hurried to keep abreast of her. "So, Garland said he dropped the parts at your house yesterday. I'm busy now waiting for Carl to wake up, but I could come to your place later and help you get started on your Astral thing."

Emma halted in her tracks. "I thought we went through this before. I won't be requiring any assistance on my project. Don't you remember?"

Archibald shrugged nonchalantly. "I might remember something like that. I guess I was hoping you'd changed your mind."

Emma sighed and looked up at the sky.

"Please, Aunt Emma. I'm bored as heck and you're one of the most interesting people I know. I really want to help you."

There was an earnest aspect to Archibald's gumption that appealed to Emma's softer side. Although she suspected before she spoke that she would regret her words later, she said, "Let's not talk here. Remember, it's a private project. But if you want to stop by and chat, I'll be home."

"Great. Thanks," Archibald said quickly. He threw a furtive glance over his shoulder and added, "Don't worry, my lips are zipped. Ants in my pants or a stick up my nose: I won't breathe a single word about your invention to anybody."

Emma was hardly reassured by Archibald's claim. Still, she smiled and shook his hand.

Archibald's face was the first thing Carl saw when he awoke from his nap. He blinked, yawned, then frowned dourly and allowed, "I must have dozed off for a minute or two."

"More like a couple of hours," replied Archibald. "Anyway, you're awake now. Hopefully in a better mood than yesterday."

Carl said something that sounded like "Ugh."

"Ugh what?"

"Just ugh. I don't feel like talking about it."

"Why not? You said that yesterday," Archibald argued.

Carl's face abruptly came alive. His eyes flashed with anger and he snapped in an annoyed voice, "Don't pester me, Arch. I'm not in the mood for it. Do you follow?"

Archibald was stunned. Carl had never attacked him verbally before. Now he knew that something was seriously wrong. He cast an anguished look at Carl and said, "Sorry. Mom says I was born nosy. Sometimes I get carried away."

Carl could see that he'd hurt Archibald's feelings, and that made him feel rotten. "Don't take it personal. Okay? I've got a lot on my mind right now. That's all."

"I understand," Archibald said timidly. "I'll just check back another time. Maybe then you'll want to talk."

"Maybe," Carl muttered. He crossed his arms over the top of his chest and stared forlornly at the ceiling.

Archibald turned to leave and swore under his breath: "Sometimes it doesn't pay to care about people."

Easygoing though it was, Willow County existed in the real world and some of its residents were occasionally distressed over personal matters. Usually no more than one person in the county was troubled on any given day, yet during the final week in June, four different Willowites were caught in the throes of despondent uncertainty.

There was Carl—afraid his sister would not appear in his dreams again and unable to remember his promise to her.

There was Archibald—upset by the way Carl had treated him.

There was Leopold—harboring doubts about *The Comprehensive Guide*, worried that his life's work had been all for naught.

And there was Warren Robinson, who had joined the troubled group when Holly left for Queen's Playland. No matter how he viewed her parting words—"Unless one of my costars sweeps me off my feet, I'll miss you too"—he was not pleased with the implications.

During the heat of midday Warren and Emmet were lounging under an apple tree on the ridge at Dither Farm. Warren was generally a self-reliant fellow who preferred to deal privately with his own problems. He was definitely not the type to cry on someone's shoulder, so to speak. But today he was feeling so weird about things, he turned to Emmet for advice. "Will you promise not to laugh if I ask you something about Holly?"

Emmet was surprised by the question, yet he heard the anxiety in Warren's voice and replied tactfully, "I won't laugh. I know how tricky girl stuff can be."

Warren hesitated for a moment, then asked, "Do you think Holly is fickle?"

Emmet grinned but did not laugh. "No, Warren, I don't *think* Holly is fickle; I *know* she is."

Warren grimaced. Although it was the answer he'd been expecting, it hurt to hear his suspicions confirmed.

Emmet could see that Warren was crestfallen and in need of some sound advice. "Listen, buddy," Emmet said sympathetically. "If I were you, I wouldn't count on Holly being too dependable. And don't get me wrong when I say this—I mean, she's my sister and I'd protect her in a fight—but she has a habit of making selfish decisions. I don't think she can help it."

Warren stiffened. "You make her sound like a monster."

Emmet waited until some of Warren's tension subsided before replying, "Holly isn't a monster, but she will drive you nuts if you let her. Basically, Holly thinks of Holly first—then she thinks of other people's feelings. I will admit, in the end she usually makes the right choices. It's just getting from A to Z with her that poses a problem."

Warren knew that Emmet was speaking the truth. Holly was Holly and there was nothing he could do about that. He drew a deep breath and stared for a moment at the glaring sun. It was time to bounce back; he was too young to have his summer ruined by a fickle girl. He sighed, and said to Emmet, "If your offer still stands, I think I'm ready to join your act."

Emmet beamed with joy. He'd been waiting weeks for Warren to come to his senses. "Welcome aboard, partner."

Warren was surprised at how tremendously relieved he was by his decision. He jumped to his feet and began to laugh. "Watch this," he shouted. Then, with a surge of energy, he threw his arms behind his head, kicked his feet out from beneath himself and hurled his body backward. *Thump-thump* went his feet as he landed on the ground.

"Wow. A backflip," Emmet cried excitedly. "I'm sure we can work that into the act somewhere."

Warren swept the hair from his face and grinned.

"Man, this is great," Emmet mused happily. "We're going to be stage partners. Can you sing?"

"Nope," Warren said flatly. "Not even in a bucket."

"Hmm. Oh well." Emmet shrugged. "So . . . the first thing we need is a name for ourselves. Since we're just starting out, we're going to want something catchy."

Warren nodded thoughtfully. "Let's see. There's you. There's me. And there's Senator."

"An unlikely trio if there ever was one," Emmet muttered. "That's good."

"What?"

" 'The Unlikely Trio.' It sounds catchy to me."

Emmet considered for a moment before replying, "You know, Warren, that's not a bad idea. Not bad at all."

Emma Bean had been meditating for an hour when Archibald found her sitting cross-legged on the carriage-house floor. She did not hear him approach and became aware of his presence only when he announced in her ear, "I'm here."

A jolt of energy shot up Emma's spine, and her eyes flew open. It took her a moment to find her voice. "Archibald."

"Are you stuck?"

"No, I'm meditating. Or at least I was before you snuck in here and startled me," Emma said more sharply than she wished. This was not a pleasant way to end an hour of meditation. She straightened her legs and gestured for Archibald to join her on the floor. "Make yourself comfortable. Let's talk."

Archibald dropped onto the plank floor and pantomimed stretching out on a bed.

Emma was not amused. She had been nurturing her idea for an Astral Projector for many years, and the project was particularly dear to her heart. She wondered if Archibald was mature enough to appreciate its potential value. The last thing she needed was a comic assistant. "Arch, if your only motive in helping me is because you're bored and looking for something fun to do, you'd better look elsewhere. I'm not playing games here."

Archibald sat up and stared soberly at his aunt. "Sorry. I was just trying to relax. I'd probably be more serious if I knew what you were planning. I mean, I've seen the drawing, but what is an Astral Projector? What does it do?"

Emma pursed her lips and studied Archibald for a moment. She knew that as soon as she answered his questions, she would be accepting him as an assistant. She could do worse, she reflected. After all, Archibald had successfully invoked the *hoche haumdoo* chant when Warren was sick with swamp fever, and he had also experienced textile aviation. So to a degree, he'd already been exposed to alternative realities. "What does an Astral Projector do?" Emma reiterated his inquiry, then answered, "It may or may not do anything, but it was designed as a resonating instrument for projecting ionic frequencies into the astral plane."

Archibald didn't speak. The look on his face said: *What?*

Emma smiled patiently and explained. "It's complicated. I'll try to put it simply. First, the astral plane is a supersensible substance, or realm, that exists above this world that we know. It's not heaven, but actually a band of refined energy hovering between earth and heaven. Many theologians believe it's where our ghost-spirits live." Emma paused to see if Archibald was following her. He was watching her alertly. "Every individual emanates unique brain frequencies that are subtly identifiable and different from those of other individuals. I hope to use the invention to project my particular frequencies into the astral plane. Of course, we'll have to wait and see if it works."

Archibald was awestruck. Some of the details were beyond him, but he was able to grasp the gist of Emma's plan. "You're absolutely amazing. I always said you were smarter than Leopold."

"Thanks for the compliment," said Emma. "But let's wait and see what happens before going that far."

A look of joyous expectation spread over Archibald's face. "So, does this mean I'm your partner?"

"As long as you remember that this is a top-secret endeavor."

"I will," Archibald declared adamantly. "Like I told you before, my lips are zipped."

Emma nodded appreciatively and rose stiffly to her feet. Sitting cross-legged on the floor wasn't as easy for her as it once had been. "Come on. Let's go to the kitchen. I need a cup of tea, and I bet you're hungry."

"How'd you know?" Archibald asked as he jumped up to follow his one-in-a-million aunt.

"Just a hunch," said Emma.

Chapter Six

Although the prospect of a week by the sea kept Leopold from falling into the depths of depression, he remained dissatisfied with *The Comprehensive Guide* and, by extension, unhappy with himself. On Monday evening, when Emma told him she had arranged a beach house for him and Matilda, he acknowledged her efforts with a glum dip of his head.

On Wednesday afternoon Leopold walked to Dither Farm to speak with Clementine about Matilda joining him at the beach. He wanted to clear the idea with Clementine before mentioning it to Matilda. As he drew near to the farm, his mood brightened at the thought that Clementine might have recently baked a pie and would be offering him a slice. Or two. Such a gracious hostess.

Sure enough, as Leopold entered through the back door of the house, he caught a whiff of hot cherry pie coming out of the oven. His nose quivered excitedly and he hurried to the kitchen.

Clementine turned at the sound of shuffling feet and greeted her guest with a delighted smile. A major benefit of living in Willow County was being surprised by people like Leopold. "Sit," she said, motioning to a chair. "You're just in time for pie."

"I was hoping for pie. Imagine that," Leopold replied with the eager grin of a child. He was immensely fond of Clementine. He admired her beauty and viewed her as the sensible matriarch of the county's most colorful family. He also respected her savvy in running a profitable cider business.

For her part, Clementine had looked up to Leopold since she was a child, and she held him in high regard. She was especially grateful to him for the role he'd played in rescuing Archibald from the kidnappers two years ago.

Leopold blessed his stomach with three slices of cherry pie before pushing away from the table and broaching the subject of his trip. In short, he told Clementine why, where, and when he was going to the beach, then implied that Emma had insisted he take Matilda. When he was done speaking, Clementine replied that she wished to consult with Henry before granting her permission.

That evening, after putting Angeline to bed, Clementine joined Henry in the parlor. "Leopold came for a visit today. He ate half a pie and announced that he was going to Virginia Beach for a week without Emma."

"The old rooster," Henry laughed. "Married one year and he's already flying the coop."

Clementine was not humored by Henry's remark. "Emma

Bean has made arrangements for a house. He wants Matilda to go with him."

Henry's laughter promptly evaporated. "Matilda is only twelve. Can we count on Leopold to steer her clear of trouble?"

"Matilda is not my worry," countered Clementine. "I'm concerned about Leopold. You know the way his mind wanders. He's safe here in the county because everybody knows him, but Virginia Beach is a crowded, modern place and I'm not sure how well he will cope. I believe Emma is worried too. She's the one who suggested he take Matilda."

"I see," said Henry, not bothering to voice an opinion. He correctly presumed that Clementine had already made a decision.

Clementine shifted in her seat and sighed. "Matilda had better go. It'd be irresponsible of us to let Leopold go alone."

Archibald's patience was beginning to wear thin on Thursday morning when he started from the farm toward Aylor's Store. He'd been to see Carl for the last four days in a row, and on each visit the big guy had refused to tell him what was wrong or even to participate in a conversation. As frustrating as the situation was for Archibald, he maintained an even temper. Carl was growing gloomier by the day, and Archibald knew that getting mad would serve no useful purpose.

One glance at Carl and Archibald knew that matters had not improved. "Hey, Carl," said Archibald, doing his best to sound cheerful.

"Arch," replied Carl, looking shamefully at the floor. He was embarrassed by his grief, and had it been less severe, he would have pretended that all was well. As it was, he couldn't muster the energy to conceal his deep sadness.

"Carl . . . it's bad, isn't it? I can tell. Something terrible is eating you inside."

"Yes," Carl answered grimly. Stella had always lived in the innermost chamber of his heart, and the idea of his passing through the long nights of his future without the chance of her visiting again filled him with dread. It felt as if someone had bored a hole in his chest and stuffed it with broken glass.

Archibald could feel the pain emanating from Carl as if it was a tangible force, and he felt compelled to somehow reach through the suffering shield. His instincts told him to reach softly and slowly. "I'm not going to push you to talk, Carl. You will when you're ready, and I'll wait a year if I have to. But keep this in mind, I have only one best friend in the world. No matter what is wrong, I'm not going to give up on you."

Carl lifted his gaze and peered solemnly yet thankfully at his young friend. He spoke in a voice that seemed strangely small to be coming from his large body. "You're a light in a tunnel."

Now it was Archibald's turn to lower his eyes. He was honored. After a moment he looked up. "Maybe tomorrow, or the day after. I'll just keep checking, Carl. You may want to talk soon."

"Maybe. I might," Carl said with a heavy sigh.

Archibald's journey from the store to the Hillacre estate was a slow and contemplative one. Carl's mental problem seemed to be taking a toll on his physical health. He had not looked well, and Archibald was worried about what might happen if he continued to decline. Archibald sensed that if he was going to help Carl, he'd better do so soon. But how, when Carl wouldn't even tell him what was wrong?

Archibald's troubled mind shifted into a lighter mode as the old Hillacre house on the hill came into view. He had spent much of the previous day helping Emma measure and lay out the materials for the Astral Projector, so he reasonably assumed that today they would begin construction. Yet it was not to be: When he arrived at the carriage house, he saw a note on the door. It was addressed to him, and it said: *"Got a headache. No work today. E. Bean."*

Archibald thought he would cry. First Carl, and now this. He was only nine—life was supposed to be fun, not a steady stream of disappointments. He bit his bottom lip and wandered back down the hill, where he spent the next three hours sitting alone by the side of Weeping Willow Swamp.

Meanwhile, back on Dither Farm, Emmet, Warren, and Senator were in the field behind the apple orchard practicing acrobatics. Having decided to call themselves "The Unlikely Trio," they were working on a repertoire of routines to go with the name. There was Emmet's juggling act, and Warren had agreed to learn stilt-walking, but they knew they needed more. Much more.

It was becoming rapidly clear that broad-shouldered Warren had a knack for acrobatics. He wasn't nearly as agile as his tumbling partner, Senator, yet he was strong, quick, and seemingly fearless. Already he and Senator had worked out a routine with double handstands, coordinated backflips, and high, swooping tosses. Of course, it was the monkey that always got tossed.

After several hours of sweaty exertion the boys went to cool off in the creek that ran below the house. It wasn't deep enough for a proper dip, but they could lie comfortably on the bottom and let the current sweep over them. Senator was disgruntled after the long practice and had retreated to the tree house.

The boys had been submerged for about ten minutes when Emmet informed his partner, "Warren, I'm proud of the way you got control of yourself and quit fretting about Holly."

"Hmph" was Warren's response. The truth was, he'd continued to torment himself privately with doubts about Holly's fidelity.

Fortunately for Warren, he was not at Queen's Playland on Thursday night when Holly and Beaufort B. Beaumont stopped in the Thane's Treat restaurant for a milk shake.

It was eight o'clock, thirty minutes before closing time at the Thane's Treat. Holly and Beaufort had just come from their first full dress rehearsal. Holly was wearing a starched white blouse and ankle-length skirt befitting a pioneer woman. Beneath the skirt were bloomers. She had removed her bonnet and hung it casually around her neck. Beaufort was attired in an 1870s U.S. Army jacket. The polished brass buttons of the uniform matched his curly copper-colored hair, and the trim of his jacket complemented his azure-blue eyes.

By design, the Wild West show was more of a spectacle than a plot-driven drama. The cast consisted of five cowboys, four Indians, three soldiers, and three pioneer women. The roles were stereotypical. Rather than acting, the performers concentrated on stunt riding, pratfalls, roping, and hollering at the top of their lungs. The story line was simple. Holly played a pioneer woman taken hostage by a band of lawless cowboys, and for the second successive year Beaufort was cast as the daring young corporal who single-handedly saves the damsel from her kidnappers. In a variation on the standard Wild West fare, the Indians led the corporal to the cowboy hideout.

Beaufort held open the door to the restaurant and suggested an isolated booth in the rear of the building.

"Sitting in the back suits me fine," Holly demurred. The longer she spent in Beaufort B. Beaumont's company, the more pronounced her Southern accent became. "I suppose we'll have enough of the crowds next week when we open the show."

"Oh gosh, we'll be mobbed constantly," Beaufort concurred. He was sixteen and highly ambitious, which made him an ideal professional match for Holly. His desire for stardom was even vaster than hers.

As Holly settled in the booth, she recalled her mother's story of the first time Henry had taken her to Nora Cook's luncheonette for a milk shake. Although Clementine's version of the occasion was always told as a comedy, Holly drew giddy comparisons between it and her current circumstances. Of course, she knew it was way too early to reach any conclusions, yet she could not refrain from thinking that Clementine and Henry had eventually gotten married.

After they ordered, Beaufort propped his elbows on the table and leaned forward. "Holly," he said in an intimate tone. "I've been wondering something that I want to ask you."

Holly tensed. She could feel Beaufort's eyes caressing her face, and she sensed he was about to pose an important question. She giggled uneasily. "Funny you should say that, Beaufort. I've been wondering something too."

"Oh?"

"What does the *B.* in your name stand for?"

Beaufort smiled in a debonair fashion. "You're not the first girl that's asked me that."

"I never suspected I was," said Holly.

Beaufort paused for effect, then said in an ostensibly modest tone, "My full name is Beaufort Braxton Beaumont. Feel free to laugh if you wish."

"Why should I laugh?" Holly said quickly. "It's a beautiful name altogether."

"You really think so?" asked Beaufort. Although he pretended to be embarrassed, he was actually pleased to have the attention focused on him.

"Absolutely," replied Holly. "Now, what were you wondering?"

"Well . . . I was wondering if you have a fella?"

At that moment the waitress appeared with their order. Holly grabbed a straw and tested her milk shake for flavor. She signaled her approval with a smile, then answered the question that was hanging in the air. "No, I don't believe I have a fella."

Beaufort tucked a napkin in his shirt, stirred his shake with a spoon, and declared, "That's a surprise. As pretty and talented as you are, I figured every boy in Willow County would be camping out on your porch."

"I didn't say I was without admirers, Beaufort. I said I don't believe I have a fella."

"Touché," Beaufort said with a wink. "I've always liked witty girls the most."

Holly blushed and chewed on her straw. On the one hand

she was flattered by her costar; yet on the other she was aware that her answer to him had not been entirely forthright. In the least, she should have mentioned Warren. Suddenly—as if to underscore her duplicity—Warren's legal guardian, Flea Jenfries, appeared in the restaurant and approached the back booth. It was evident from her stride and the expression on her face that she had not come to eat. Ignoring Beaufort, she informed Holly in an angry tone, "I've been looking for you. You were supposed to be home for supper."

"Gee, Flea, I'm sorry," Holly gushed. "I meant to tell you I'd be a little late today. It must have slipped my mind."

Although Flea was physically small for a grown woman, there was nothing diminutive about the force of her personality. In her own precise way, she could be as intimidating as any authority carrying a badge and a gun. It was with apparent restraint that Flea now glared at Holly.

"Flea, I said I was sorry," Holly reiterated defensively.

Beaufort, a graduate of the school of Southern manners, stood and gestured at the seat beside him. "Excuse me, ma'am. We've not yet been introduced. My name is Beaufort B. Beaumont, and I suspect you're Holly's mother."

"I am not," Flea said definitively. "I'm Holly's chaperon."

"All the same"—Beaufort dipped his head—"would you care to join us for a beverage?"

"I would not. Holly, you have sixty seconds to finish your milk shake and meet me outside."

"Yes, Flea."

"Fifty-nine and counting," Flea noted as she departed.

"Do pardon the interruption," Holly said with self-conscious distress as she slid out of the booth. "I'd better go now."

"Oh, that's right, you're fourteen. Yes, you should do what your chaperon says."

Holly hesitated for a second and stared at Beaufort. She wanted to ask what he meant by his remark, but she didn't have time to hear his answer.

"See you tomorrow," Beaufort said with a small laugh. "And don't worry about the check. I'll take care of that."

On Friday when Emma Bean checked the mailbox she was pleased to see a manila envelope postmarked Washington, D.C. In the left-hand corner she saw an *S* scribbled over a National Security Council emblem. She ripped open the package and read the cover letter.

Emma Bean,

I am a bean for letting you coerce me into this. I expect you to send me original negatives and all copies of film. Direct to my desk. Mark package confidential.

Key fits front door of three-bedroom house on map.

Daily maid service. Food and beverages not supplied.

Instruct spouse to tell curious neighbors that house belongs to Uncle Bill. Available Monday, June 29, to Monday, July 6.

Send film pronto.

Roger Simmons

Emma was still chortling moments later when she found her husband in the Inner Sanctum. Leopold looked up from his papers and asked, "Pleased with yourself, or someone else?"

"Myself. I just hoodwinked an old colleague."

"Proud of you, dear. How'd you do that?"

"By threatening him with a film I never made. Good man, he's offered to lend you a beach house for a week."

Leopold raised his brow. He was impressed. "Fabulous. When do I ship out?"

"Monday morning. There's a bus out of Bricksburg at nine A.M. If you ask, I'm sure Henry will drive you and Matilda."

Leopold pushed his chair back and rested his feet on the table. "Ah, the sea," he mused longingly. "Soon I'll be soaking in the sea. Lucky me."

Part Two

Chapter Seven

The longer one observes the rhythms of life, the more one notices that certain days are simply more important than others. One day is filled with portent, while the next is practically void of significance. Such is the relative nature of days.

Although Monday, June 29, was not a critical day for every single person from Willow County, it was a turning point for many people in this story.

For Holly, it was two days before the Wild West show opened to the public. More importantly, it was the day Beaufort asked her to be his girl. She was in the air-conditioned stables tending to Dan's silky coat when Beaufort approached the stall and voiced the unexpected request. He did so casually and without preamble, almost as if he were asking to borrow a broom. Holly hesitated. Beaufort had been solicitous toward her for the last few days, yet there was something about his informal approach that made her uneasy. She allowed that she was just a Willow County girl—not exactly sure how things were done in the wider world—still, she followed her own instincts and told him she would need a few days to consider the offer.

"Why, Holly?" Beaufort pressed. "What's to think about?"

Holly stopped brushing Dan for a moment and flashed a critical glance at her costar. "There's lots to think about. I'm not the type to jump into things. Asking me to be your girl is a serious matter."

Beaufort was surprised. He'd been expecting her to swoon and give him an immediate yes. Now he wasn't sure how to react. His previous experiences with girls had taught him little about rejection. "Hmph. Well . . . so that's it, then," Beaufort mumbled ambivalently.

Holly had reservations, but she wasn't a fool. She knew that sophisticated guys like Beaufort didn't appear on the horizon every day. "Beaufort." She said the name tenderly. "I'm touched by your offer, and I would have said no if I wasn't interested in considering it. I'm only asking for a few days to think."

"Yes, of course," Beaufort replied in a clipped tone. He was anxious to maintain his composure.

For Matilda and Leopold, Monday was an exciting day. In the morning they rode the bus to Virginia Beach and settled into their government-owned residence. It was a typical beach house, with wall-to-wall carpeting, rattan furniture, and corny art in the bathrooms. The main appeal of the place was location; it was four blocks from the ocean. In the afternoon Leopold and Matilda ventured out to the boardwalk to purchase the basic necessities for a week at the beach: flip-flops, hats, sunscreen, sunglasses, magazines, and two durable inflatable rafts. The outing was an eye-opening experience for Leopold. He was shocked by the fashions. Not in his wildest dreams had he imagined how skimpy a modern bikini could be.

For Garland Barlow, the last Monday in June was an inspired day. Much to the curiosity of his assistants, Garland locked the door to his cluttered office, drew the shades, and hunched over a notepad for three hours. Below lies the result of his labor. (The reader should keep in mind that Garland was a mechanic by trade, not a poet.)

Bit by a Flea

I've got an itch
That needs scratching.
I've been bit by a Flea.
It might be contagious,
Or maybe I'm the only one
Allergic. Why me?
It's worse than a rash
Or a boil or a whelp.
It itches like crazy.
I need help.
It's a shivering tingle
That tickles all over.
It won't let me be.

For Emmet and Warren, Monday was a day of vision. During the heat of the afternoon they were in the tree fort discussing their lack of professional prospects when Emmet conceived the notion of renting the Binkerton town hall and producing their own show. "If no one else will hire us," he reasoned, "we'll hire ourselves."

Warren endorsed the suggestion enthusiastically. "That's the ticket! We could be ready by the end of summer."

"If we work hard, we will be," said Emmet. With Warren's support, Emmet moved directly into the planning stage. "We're going to need an opening act. Tomorrow let's hitchhike to King County and see if Contessa has trained her pig yet. Senator can come with us and say hi to Rosey."

Warren was hesitant. "Shouldn't we wait and see if the town hall is available before we start lining up outside acts?"

Emmet wasn't listening. "If the pig isn't ready, maybe Contessa can sing."

Warren shrugged with resignation. He knew that once Emmet had made up his mind to go after something, there was no use trying to talk him out of it.

Senator, who had been watching the boys converse, picked his nose and scratched his furry stomach. For him, June 29 was just another day.

Monday was a critical day for Carl. It had started before dawn, when Stella had visited him in a dream. He was initially elated to see that she had not faded from existence, but then, when she appealed to him to honor his childhood promise to her, his high spirits sank under a wave of self-reproach. He had no idea what she was talking about—he could not remember making any promises to her. He knew he'd probably done so, and Carl, being the kind of person he was, blamed himself for the lapse in memory and poured guilt onto the pile of misery he already harbored inside.

He had reached the point where he could no longer bear his burden alone. It was time for him to confide in Archibald. For that, Carl wanted privacy, so he wheeled his customized seat onto the store porch and parked in a corner to wait for his loyal friend.

Archibald had arisen at his usual hour. After dressing and eating a slice of toast, he headed to the store. He wasn't very optimistic about the prospect of Carl being ready to talk (the big guy had disappointed him for the past seven days in a row). He was going out of habit, and because he wanted Carl to know he cared.

Archibald did a double take when he saw Carl sitting in a shady corner of the store porch. As Archibald was about to discover, the twenty-ninth of June was a day for revelations. He approached without a word and hopped onto the porch railing across from Carl. The moment was clearly portentous. There was no need for idle greetings.

Carl waited until Archibald was comfortably settled, then reached into one of his shirt pockets and withdrew a photograph. "Here," he said, handing the old picture to Archibald. "You better have a look at this before I tell you what I have to say."

Archibald glanced questioningly at Carl before turning his attention to the emulsified image on the paper in his hand. He saw a young boy and girl standing on a porch in front of a large building. After three seconds Archibald looked up and asked in an incredulous voice, "Carl, is that you?"

"Yeah," Carl confirmed. "And the girl standing beside me was my twin sister."

"Twin sister?" Archibald could hardly fathom the thought. He studied the photograph again. The children in the picture were his age or a little older. The girl stared straight at the camera. She had long hair, high cheekbones, and a thin, knowing smile on her face. She was beautiful. Her smile sent a shiver through Archibald.

"Her name was Stella."

"Was?"

Carl coughed and cleared his throat. "Stella died when she was eleven."

Archibald nearly fell backward off the rail.

Carl's voice threatened to crack into a cry as he told Archibald, "Losing Stella was the worst thing that ever happened to me. There hasn't been a day since that I didn't feel like a part of me was missing."

Archibald was unsure of what to say in a situation like this, so he said what he felt in his heart. "I'm so so sorry for you, Carl. You must have loved her, didn't you?"

Carl bit his trembling bottom lip.

"Do you have any other brothers or sisters?"

Carl blew air through his nostrils. "No. At least none that I know of. Stella and I were orphans."

"Orphans?" Archibald mouthed the word silently. Carl's story was going from sad to devastating. (Archibald's family frustrated him regularly, but he couldn't imagine life without them.) He was too discombobulated to speak.

"Being an orphan wasn't the end of the world," mumbled Carl. He thought, but did not add: *Or it wasn't until I lost Stella.*

Archibald swallowed and studied the photograph again. Carl's eyes were on his sister. Although he was taller and larger boned than Stella, she appeared to be the confident one. Indeed, there was something cocky about her stance.

"There's more," said Carl, breaking the uneasy silence that had built up in the corner. Then he told Archibald how Stella had been coming to him in dreams throughout the years since she had died. Carl spoke of Stella's recent announcement that she was fading away and would soon stop visiting him, and he told Archibald about the forgotten promise she had asked him to honor.

Archibald's mouth had fallen open while Carl told his story. He made no effort to close it when Carl was done. He just sat on the railing and stared at his friend in sorrowful amazement.

On Monday evening Jimmy Aylor and Felton Fibbs were at the checkout counter playing backgammon for a penny a point when a black Mercedes Benz pulled into the store parking lot. The car had tinted windows and New York licence plates. The driver's door opened and a stranger stepped into view. He was wearing a dark suit and sunglasses. He flicked a cigarette on the ground, ran a comb through his gelled hair, and started into the store. The man stopped in the doorway, looked around as if he owned the place, then nodded and said, "Hello, Jimmy. Hi, Felton. How ya doing?"

Jimmy looked at Felton and Felton looked at Jimmy. Neither of them could identify the curious customer.

"Nice to see some things never change," said the stranger as he casually inspected the premises.

Jimmy mumbled something that only Felton could hear.

The man peered down the center aisle and laughed. "I'll be damned. I see Carl is still here."

Just then Henry Dither materialized in the doorway. Until this moment June 29 had been a typical day for Henry. That was about to change. He noticed Jimmy's tension and stopped just inside the store. When he turned to eye the source of that tension, the stranger grinned and said, "Henry, you old dog."

Henry couldn't see past his own reflection in the man's

dark glasses, but he had the odd feeling that he'd heard the strident voice before.

When the stranger's grin gave way to a guffaw and he removed his sunglasses, Henry recognized him in a flash. "I'll be a duck if it isn't Marvin Jinks!"

"I was starting to wonder if anybody would remember me."

"I remember," Henry said with dubious innuendo. Years ago, before he married Clementine, he had teamed up with Marvin Jinks for a couple of rebellious weeks. At one blurry point in their shenanigans they had spent a few hours in a bar near Binkerton called the Hot Spot. Their patronage of the place had ended violently, with Henry lying on the ground outside the door. When he woke up fifteen hours later, he was looking out a bus window at the interior wall of the Port Authority terminal in midtown Manhattan. Marvin and Henry had bummed around the city for three days before Henry called it quits and returned to Willow County. Marvin had loved the place and stayed. Fourteen years after they parted, Henry had spotted Marvin in a movie called *One Fell Swoop*.

"What's the matter?" Marvin asked lightly.

"Nothing. I just never expected to see you again," Henry admitted. "So, if that's your fancy car outside, you must be a big movie star now."

Marvin laughed. "I was in a couple of movies, as a favor for a friend, but I haven't acted for years."

"What do you do for a living?" interjected Jimmy. He was fast developing a theory that Marvin had criminal connections.

"I'm a literary agent," Marvin said proudly. "In fact, I'm an associate at the Earl Slide Literary Agency. I've driven down here to speak with Leopold Hillacre about a book he wrote."

Henry, Felton, and Jimmy exchanged quick glances. They were well aware of *The Comprehensive Guide*.

Suddenly Henry remembered something about Marvin. "Excuse me for saying so, but I seem to recollect that you couldn't read."

Marvin was not offended. "I can read a bit. I just don't make a habit of it. Besides, I'm an agent, not a publisher. All I really do is take people to lunch and be friendly."

"You make a living doing that?" Henry asked doubtfully.

Marvin nodded. "Yep. A pretty good one, too."

Henry raised his eyebrows and rubbed his chin. It seemed as if he would never cease to be amazed by the modern world.

Chapter Eight

On Tuesday morning, after obtaining Clementine's permission to spend the day in Binkerton, Emmet, Warren, and Senator left the farm and walked to where Route 631 met Route 628. Although Emmet knew their ultimate destination was King County, not Binkerton, he suffered only a minor twinge of guilt about the deception. After all, he was not being unveracious; he was merely exercising a liberal interpretation of the truth.

While they were waiting for a vehicle to appear, Emmet and Warren decided that if their first ride terminated in Binkerton, they would go by the town hall and see Eugenna White. Eugenna was the mayor's administrative assistant. Through the years she had slowly yet surely taken charge of every key that fit a lock on town property.

It was a sunny day and the boys were glad they had worn

caps. Senator had no cap, but he didn't care. He was a smart enough monkey to squat in the pool of shade behind Warren.

Patience was the name of the game when hitchhiking in Willow County. After approximately an hour a large farm truck rumbled around the bend. It decreased speed and creaked to a halt about twenty yards beyond the Unlikely Trio. As they darted toward the truck, their senses were assaulted by the pungent odor of hot manure and the chorusing of nervous chickens.

Emmet ran forward to confer with the driver. The man had a beaked nose, a tiny mouth, a shortened forehead, and a sharply descending widow's peak. He looked as if he had been born to haul feathered fowl.

"Thanks for stopping," Emmet said with a polite tip of his cap. "We're heading to King County, just over the bridge."

Either the man couldn't talk or he wasn't in the mood. He nodded and motioned toward the back of the truck.

"Can you let us off at the Pamunkey River?" asked Emmet.

The man nodded again and reached for the gearshift.

Emmet hurried to the rear of the truck, where Warren and Senator stood holding their noses. "Quick, get on."

Warren and Senator glared dubiously at Emmet.

"Now," Emmet urged, hoisting himself onto the tailgate as the truck lurched forward. "A little smell won't hurt you."

Reluctantly Warren, and then Senator, jumped aboard as the truck pulled away. The chickens (which had never seen a monkey before) somehow gathered the impression that they were under attack, and they responded in noisy unison. Chickens can be as excessive as sheep when it comes to collective fear, and they demonstrated this fact by squawking all the way to the Pamunkey River bridge.

• • •

Emma Bean was an independent thinker who had dedicated her life to the pursuit of anything and everything that fascinated her. And she was bold. When she was younger, she had traveled the world, seeing as much if not more of the planet than Marco Polo. Psychologically she was without limitations. Mentally she was plain old smart. She loved exposing mysteries—once she decided to unmask one, she would tug tenaciously at its veils until light fell upon the subject. It was the bulldog approach to analytical thinking: Basically, she would bite the nose of any conundrum she faced and not let go until it pooped out and surrendered.

Whatever intellectual process Emma used (real genius cannot be explained and we will never know the mental gymnastics she performed before conceiving her invention), the idea for her Astral Projector was based upon the inherent qualities of a tuning fork. Yes: She was inspired by a pronged metal implement that gives a fixed tone when struck. Somehow, she combined the image of a tuning fork with her knowledge of psychic vibrations and designed a transmitter for broadcasting into the astral plane.

For centuries, sadhus, saints, and assorted mystics from the East had attempted to project their mental frequencies into the astral plane. Yet they had done so only after years of disciplined meditation. Emma was taking a thoroughly Western approach. She was building a machine for the job.

Emma's machine was designed as a 104-inch-tall pyramid-shaped brass structure surrounded by spirals of twisted copper wire. Hollow inside, it contained a metal swing suspended 28 inches off the ground. A piezoelectric crystal was mounted at the apex.

Caution: Unless you have been trained in transcendental displacement kinetics, do not attempt to build one of these at home.

Around midmorning on Tuesday, Archibald and Emma screwed together the base of the Astral Projector and set it in the middle of the carriage house beneath a skylight. As they worked, Archibald told his aunt about Carl and Stella, and about the dreams Carl had been having. Emma listened to Archibald with great interest and was not totally surprised when he asked her to repeat what she had told him about ghost-spirits living in the astral plane. In fact, Emma was rather impressed that Archibald had made the connection. "Yes," she said. "The astral plane is where transcended spirits reside. Yet the full truth is . . . well, the astral plane isn't an actual place—a place with a map that you can touch. It's more abstract. More theoretical. In a way, you might say it's a place that only exists in the mind of the beholder."

Archibald was baffled. "You mean you made it up?"

"No, it's there," Emma said with a benign twinkle in her eye. "But to find it, you have to believe what you behold."

Archibald paused to weigh his thoughts. A question was forming on his lips when he and Emma were distracted by a shadow in the doorway. Emma hastily tossed a tarp over the parts of her invention and whirled to face the intruder. "Who are you and what do you want?"

Marvin Jinks had been living in New York City for fifteen years and was inured to brusque behavior. He inclined his head to Emma and said politely, "Pardon me. My name is Marvin Jinks. I'm associated with the Earl Slide Literary Agency on Fifth Avenue in New York City. I was hoping to speak with Leopold Hillacre."

Emma assessed Marvin with a look and said wryly, "Leopold is away on vacation. You should've made an appointment."

"I would have if you had a telephone," Marvin replied.

"The Hillacres don't like phones," interjected Archibald.

Emma put a hand on Archibald's shoulder and told Marvin, "If you wish, Mr. Jinks, try again next week. Now, if you will excuse us, we're busy here."

Marvin frowned. He was an agent and agents are not so easily dismissed. "I'll be on my way as soon as you tell me where to find Mr. Hillacre. The Earl Slide agency is eager to represent your husband, and if I may say so, madam, he will need our help. Publishers can be terribly ruthless."

Emma snorted. She knew how the game was played. "Leopold is in Virginia Beach, staying in a guest house that was rented for him by Moberg, Quinn, and Associates."

"Moberg, Quinn," Marvin repeated weakly. It was the name of New York's premier literary agency, Earl Slide's main competitor. "Do you have an address?"

Emma scowled at Marvin as if irritated by an insect. "I might have heard him mention Ocean Avenue. That's all I know. You had better leave now, before my assistant gets angry. We have work to do."

"Important work," added Archibald.

Marvin bowed slightly as he backed out of the door. "I'm on my way. Thanks for your help."

At ten forty-nine the Unlikely Trio stood on the Pamunkey River bridge plucking feathers from their clothes, ears, nostrils, and hair—or fur in Senator's case. The boys had lost their caps along the way.

"At least we made it," remarked Emmet.

Warren was not feeling very philosophical. "Will you quit looking at the bright side of things!"

"Sorry," said Emmet. He moved to the bridge railing and pointed west across the river. "See that farm? Unless I'm wrong, that's where Contessa Cunningham lives."

"What do you mean, 'unless I'm wrong'?" Warren snapped.

"I've never actually been there before. But if it isn't that farm, it's the one farther down the road."

Warren moaned. Senator plucked a feather from the tip of his tail.

The picturesque farmhouse with the bright blue shutters looked empty. The shades were drawn in the windows and there was no sign of Mike Cunningham's truck. The trio stood indecisively at the yard gate. A stone sidewalk lined with well-tended flower beds led up to the front door. A platoon of ceramic elves, dwarfs, and leprechauns stood guard around the premises. Two plaster gargoyles lurked in the bushes.

"Emmet, go knock on the door," suggested Warren. "I'll wait here with Senator."

"Maybe I should have called first."

"Too late for that."

"You're right. Okay. I'm going." Emmet stepped through the gate and hesitated. He was feeling jumpy. It wasn't the strange house that intimidated him. He was unsettled by the prospect of seeing Contessa. It had been nearly three months since the last time he had basked in her radiance.

"Go on," urged Warren.

Emmet walked timidly ahead, pausing periodically to glance back at the gate for reassurance. He was halfway to the house when an eighty-pound pig charged out of nowhere. Emmet dove to his right. As he hit the ground, he noticed that the pig was wearing a pink pillbox hat. It turned, preparing to charge again. Emmet scrambled toward the nearest tree. The pig bolted after him. It was rapidly gaining ground, but halted when someone called, "Porcellina? Where are you?"

It was Emmet's poor luck that he had run toward a holly tree. He could hear Warren and Senator laughing, but he climbed the tree anyway. He wasn't taking any chances with the pig.

An instant later Contessa Cunningham appeared from behind the house. She was barefoot, wearing shorts and a crimson blouse. She carried what looked like a wand. Contessa glanced at the pig, glanced at Warren and Senator, then peered into the holly tree.

"Hello, Contessa," squeaked Emmet. "How you doing?"

"Emmet. I'm fine," replied Contessa. "I must say though, I'm surprised to see you in that tree."

"Not as surprised as I am to be here. That your pig?"

"Yes. Her name is Porcellina."

"Pretty thing," remarked Emmet. "Is she dangerous?"

"No, she's harmless. She likes to eat and play. That's all."

"Eat what?"

"Corn," answered Contessa, waving her wand at Emmet. "Now come down before you break a branch."

Emmet did as he was told, and at the same time Warren and Senator entered the yard. They followed Contessa and her pig to the back of the house, where she had set up a practice ring. They were joined by Rosey, a rhesus monkey that belonged to Mike Cunningham. It had been two years since Senator had last seen Rosey at the Binkerton Independence Festival. Although she was a short-tailed macaque from the East Indies and he was a long-tailed *Macaca mulatta* from southern Asia, they were fast friends. They chattered excitedly when they saw each other and scampered off to play by the river.

Contessa led Porcellina into the ring to show the boys what she and the pig had learned to do. It was a simple act. While Contessa played a fast jig on the xylophone, Porcellina pranced around in circles. The pig was cute, but it would be an abuse of the word to call her a dancer. She lacked finesse.

Emmet applauded when the performance was done.

Contessa curtsied and smiled.

"Can you sing?" asked Emmet.

"No, but I can dance."

Emmet shrugged. The show needed a singer and he'd been hoping Contessa could fill the slot. Still, he had not come all this way for nothing, and ignoring Warren's whispered advice to the contrary, he offered Contessa and Porcellina a ten-minute spot in their upcoming show. "We'll give you twenty percent of the profits."

"That's very generous. You've got a deal," Contessa agreed.

Emmet reached to shake her hand. "We'll start advertising as soon as we confirm a date for the town hall."

"Just let me know when the date is settled," said Contessa. "The number here is PKY-5595. I'll make posters and plaster them all over this side of King County."

Chapter Nine

For no reason at all, Henry Dither awoke an hour earlier than usual on Wednesday, July 1. He got dressed quietly so as not to arouse his sleeping wife and went downstairs to make coffee. When the brew was ready, he filled a cup and wandered out into the predawn darkness. He was surprised by how damp the air felt, and when he stooped to touch the grass, he found it covered with dew. He took a sip of coffee and started toward the ridge behind the house. He wanted to watch the sun rise over the farm.

Henry found his way through the dark and leaned against the east side of an apple tree. Moments later, as the sun began its daily ascent, Henry realized that something was wrong. The great star could barely be seen; its light was diffused by zillions of water molecules suspended in the air. For the second time this summer, a dense fog had enveloped Dither Farm.

Although Henry was intelligent, he was not a particularly

deep thinker. (He certainly wasn't an Emma Bean or a Leopold Hillacre.) He was a farmer and a family man, and he tended to see things for what they were, not what they might be. This morning he saw a world of eerie vapors. The sight dismayed him. He stood fast against the apple tree and sipped courage from his cup. Ten minutes passed, then twenty, until soon a kind of poetic prayer formed in Henry's heart: *Let life be good and the sun shine through. Let light come and drink the dew.*

Henry heard something moving in the orchard and turned just as Clementine appeared at his side. "Good morning," she said in a clear voice that seemed out of context with the fog.

Henry put an arm over Clementine's shoulder and drew her close. "It's a strange one. I don't trust this weather."

"It's nothing. It will pass."

Henry kissed his wife gently on the cheek. "I'm amazed you found me."

"Look," said Clementine, pointing east.

Henry followed the direction of her finger. Through the misty wall that surrounded them, he could see a small pocket of light illuminating a distant hill.

"Close your eyes and kiss me again. On the lips," Clementine said with a giggle.

Henry obeyed. When he was done, he saw that the pocket had expanded. "Hmmm. I better do that again."

"Suit yourself," Clementine said gaily.

Henry wrapped his arms around his wife and suited himself for three minutes. He laughed as he withdrew from the embrace and looked around. The fog was beginning to dissipate.

"Maybe you should try one more time," Clementine teased.

"Yes, yes. I believe I should."

• • •

As Marvin Jinks drove toward Virginia Beach, he thought about Leopold Hillacre. Marvin didn't know the man well (did anyone?), but he'd grown up in Willow County and had seen enough of Leopold to be confident he could spot him in a crowd. After all, Marvin reasoned, how many balding, six-foot-tall, seventy-five-year-old men with bushy eyebrows and large noses could there be on Ocean Avenue? He had to find Leopold before the old man signed with the Moberg, Quinn agency.

Virginia state troopers do not take kindly to vehicles with New York tags speeding on their highways, and they demonstrated their displeasure by giving Marvin three tickets between Richmond and Norfolk. Poorer by several hundred dollars, Marvin eventually reached Virginia Beach in the early afternoon. After driving up and down Ocean Avenue a dozen times, he parked his car and scouted the boardwalk on foot. His coat and tie made him rather conspicuous. He ignored the curious glances.

At one point Marvin looked right at Leopold without recognizing his quarry. He simply didn't think that the odd fellow with the panama hat, reflective sunglasses, and bright red trunks could possibly be the author of The Comprehensive Guide. It later occurred to Marvin to take another look at the man in the red trunks, but when he returned to the stretch of beach where he'd seen him, Marvin found no one fitting the description. Luckless Marvin: It just wasn't his day. If he had only lifted his eyes and gazed east, he would have seen two interesting people heading to sea on inflatable rafts. One was a lanky old fellow wearing goggles, and the other was a freckle-faced girl sporting a purple bathing cap.

After several harmless setbacks, Matilda and Leopold managed to negotiate their way past the incoming surf. When they were safely in the region of gentle swells, they climbed triumphantly upon their canvas conveyances. Matilda dangled her legs over the sides of her raft and enjoyed the view. Leopold clasped his hands behind his head and lay with his face to the sun.

"So, Mr. Agitated Writer," Matilda called in jest. "How do you feel now?"

"Marvelous," Leopold answered cheerfully. "There's not a thought in my head."

"That's good," observed Matilda. By chance she happened to turn toward the boardwalk just as a gull swooped down and bombed a pedestrian with a dollop of personal waste. Oddly, the defiled pedestrian was wearing a business suit. Matilda could see him shouting and shaking his fist at the sky. Although she couldn't hear what the man said, it seemed likely from the reactions of the people around him that he had used offensive language.

After paddling around for thirty minutes, Matilda informed Leopold that she was going ashore. "I'm getting burned out here," she explained. "And I'm thirsty."

Leopold did not move or say a word. Matilda thought she heard him grunt his assent before she headed back to shore. She was pleased that he was finally relaxing.

In the back of his mind Leopold was aware of the undulating motion of the sea and the warm embrace of the sun on his skin. Gently up, then gently down. It was like heaven on earth. He was relaxing indeed.

Matilda went up to the boardwalk to buy a soda. She lingered outside an arcade for a few minutes before returning to the beach. She sat on her towel, applied sunblock to her face, and glanced idly out to sea. At first she thought nothing of the blob of color she saw bobbing on the horizon. But then she recognized the blob and jumped to her feet. *"Leopold!"* she screamed. "Wake up. You're drifting. LEOPOLD!"

Leopold was indeed drifting, but in his mind it was along the soft border of dreamland; not on the open sea. When he heard a gull squawking in the distance, he thought it was a celestial trumpet. Ah, there is no finer joy than heavenly rest. To him, the sibilant sound of lapping water was generated by hundreds of baby angels flapping their little wings. Faintly, from far away, he imagined he heard someone calling his name. It pleased him that someone cared.

As Matilda was running to find a lifeguard, her sister Holly was standing in front of a full-length mirror at Queen's Playland. It was her big day; the season premier of the Wild West show was set to open in thirty minutes. After adjusting a few curls under the front of her bonnet, she hurried out of the apartment and skipped toward the stables. She had ten minutes in which to saddle Dan and meet the rest of the cast at the arena gate. In her mind she could already hear the audience gasping as she rode into view. The glory of it all! Everyone was watching the girl from Willow County. There was an explosion of wild applause, and the crowd began to chant: *Holly, Holly, oh my golly! Look at Holly go!*

Holly and Dan rendezvoused with the rest of the cast behind the arena gate and waited for Sally Swope to ring the starting bell. As Holly's excitement mounted, she was surprised to find herself thinking about Warren Robinson. She did not know why he had popped into her head at this moment— yet there he was. And with his image came a pang of guilt.

Holly had hardly given Warren a thought since leaving the farm. A moment later, when Beaufort rode up beside her and tipped his hat, Holly couldn't help but make comparisons. Both boys were handsome and broad-shouldered, and more importantly, both were attracted to her. Beaufort was definitely more sophisticated, but as Holly was starting to realize, his sophistication often served as a screen behind which he hid his true feelings. Beaufort sometimes said things that were difficult for Holly to interpret. Did he mean what he said, or was he joking? Warren, on the other hand, was easy to read. There was an earnest innocence about him that Holly found lacking in Beaufort. Still, Beaufort had style—just look at the debonair way he sat in the saddle.

Holly was jolted from her reflections by the sound of a ringing bell. It was show time!

At the same moment that Holly and Dan pranced into the arena at Queen's Playland, two burly lifeguards wrestled a rescue punt through the surf off Virginia Beach. When they were beyond the breakers, they hopped into the punt and started rowing toward the shipping lanes. That was where they had last seen the old man. The lifeguards paddled as fast as their arms would move. So far this summer, they had not lost a single tourist, and they were determined not to do so now.

A very distressed Matilda watched helplessly from the shore. Beside her stood the head lifeguard and two paramedics. They were soon surrounded by a crowd of curiosity seekers.

Meanwhile an oblivious Leopold continued to drift out to sea. Somewhere in the back of his sleeping mind he noted that he was excessively warm and wondered why his wife had turned the electric blanket on high. But then he reminded himself that he was on vacation and wasn't supposed to worry about little things.

Moments later it occurred to him that his skin was on fire, and he awoke with a start. He gasped as his eyes opened. Was that an aircraft carrier? What was it doing so close to shore? Alarmed, he rolled to his right and gasped again. He could barely discern the shapes of the buildings lining the boardwalk. When he craned his neck and looked down, he was too shocked to gasp. The water below him was aphotic, so deep it seemed black. Though it was hard for him to believe, he suddenly realized that he had drifted beyond the continental shelf.

No philosophy was required for Leopold to know he was in trouble. Forget his burning skin, forget the sudden dryness in his throat: He could hear the sea lapping at his lightweight craft, and he knew that he'd been caught in a powerful current. Scanning the horizon, he saw that he was picking up speed.

One learns much about people by observing the disparate ways in which individuals react in a crisis. Almost all of us want to live: It is the different choices one makes in seeking survival that define the person.

Leopold was frightened by the situation, but he was an old man, familiar with thoughts of his own mortality, and he didn't let his fear make him hysterical. For several minutes he tried to paddle his raft toward shore, but the current was too strong and he soon realized he was getting nowhere. A quick analysis of the circumstances informed him that his options for action were limited. He understood that he might be experiencing the final moments of his life, but what could he do about that? Flail around desperately and expend all his energy in vain, or resign himself to fate and relax? He decided to be calm. If I die, I die and that's it, he reasoned simply. And if I live, then so much the better. I might as well exercise my rational mind while the opportunity still exists.

Good old Leopold. He wasn't Willow County's most original eccentric for nothing. He dismissed the notion of trying to save himself, and began a critical review of *The Comprehensive Guide*.

As Leopold ruminated about his book, he was pleasantly surprised by how much of the work he could remember. Chapter by chapter, it all came back to him like a party of dear friends returning from a long journey. Some of them he had met fifty years before. Others were new aquaintances. He was fond of them all. They embodied the seasons of his life. Each meant something different to him. With each passing minute, Leopold delved deeper and deeper into such abstract reminiscences, until he all but forgot where he was. It was his idea of fun.

Leopold was so absorbed in his reflections that he felt a pang of annoyance when he heard the cries of the lifeguards in the approaching punt. Yet the spasm passed quickly. He was ultimately a huge proponent of survival. He sat up on his raft and hollered, "Hello. I'm here. Still alive."

Leopold would shudder in future years when he recalled how his tiny voice had been gobbled by the vast, voracious ocean.

Chapter Ten

Even before Sally Swope singled her out for praise, Holly knew she had performed flawlessly in her professional debut. She had executed all the rehearsed maneuvers on cue, in the right spot, and with panache.

"Splendid job, Holly. Such polish is rare for a beginner," Sally said in front of the cast as they gathered after the show.

"Thank you, Miss Swope," Holly responded with a gracious flutter. "Of course, I couldn't have done it without Dan."

"Take care of that pony and keep up the good work. You'll go places," Sally said with a respectful nod, before addressing the group as a whole. "I couldn't have hoped for a better opening show. It was excellent. And excellence deserves rewards. Each of you will receive ten free tokens, to be used at your discretion anywhere in the park tonight."

Prior to this moment they had been denied the pleasures of

Queen's Playland, and so now they were thrilled. Kenny Fines, one of the footsoldiers, checked to make sure he understood. "You mean we can go on any ride we want?"

"Yes," Sally said with a rare smile. "You earned it."

As the performers were leaving the pavillion, Beaufort caught up with Holly at the exit and asked in a bitter tone, "So, how does it feel to steal your first show?"

Holly was surprised by Beaufort's manner. "I didn't steal the show," she replied. "I just did my job."

Beaufort's face tightened with thinly disguised resentment. "Your job is to play a frightened woman and be grateful when I come to the rescue. You acted as if you were doing me a favor by escaping with me."

In a flash Holly understood the problem. Beaufort felt threatened. Her performance had jeopardized his status as the show's main attraction. Obviously, thought Holly, Beaufort has never worked with an equal before. And that's what I am: an equal. I didn't realize it before today myself, but now I do and so does he. He'll never admit it, of course, and there is no sense in me rubbing it in. "Don't be angry," she said with a diplomatic smile. "It's true, I may have exaggerated my gestures and gotten a little carried away with my stunts."

"A little! You were practically screaming for attention."

Holly hadn't expected such pettiness from Beaufort. When they first met, she'd thought he was just the kind of guy she had always wanted, but now . . . well, she was glad she'd hesitated when he asked her to be his girl. "It was my first show, Beaufort. Give me a break."

"Hmph."

Holly could see that Beaufort's pride needed mending, and she knew the tool for the job: flattery. "You were the reason I did so well. Working with an experienced costar like you gave me confidence."

Beaufort's expression improved slightly. "We do make an appealing team."

"The audience seemed to think so. Did you hear the applause when we rode out together?"

Beaufort nodded. "It was thunderous."

"You're probably used to it, but that was the sweetest sound I've ever heard."

Beaufort pursed his lips thoughtfully for several seconds, shrugged as if to say what's done is done, then reminded Holly, "You know I'm still waiting for an answer from you."

"I know," Holly said softly. She had her doubts, but she was not ready to dismiss Beaufort. Not yet. "And I'm still thinking. We only just met ten days ago. I, ah . . . it might be fun to meet somewhere and talk."

Beaufort looked down, then up; then noted, "The whole cast is free tonight. Surely your chaperon won't make you stay in."

Holly was quick to take his hint. "Let's meet at the Eiffel Tower at seven. I haven't been to the top yet."

"Okay. I'll be there."

"See ya then," Holly said with a comely smile before turning and hurrying home to the apartment. She could hardly wait to hear what Flea had to say about her stellar debut.

At a quarter past five, after almost three hours at sea, Leopold Hillacre was returned safely to shore. Before falling to his knees and kissing the sand, he told everyone within shouting distance that the two lifeguards were heroes. A paramedic stepped forward, laid a towel over Leopold's sunburned back, and handed him a bottle of water. The head lifeguard advised the curiosity seekers to disperse. "The old man has had a fright. He's going to be fine, but he doesn't need a lot of strangers gawking at him."

As if to prove the lifeguard's point, Leopold stood and waved gamely to the crowd. That is when he noticed Matilda eyeing him angrily. "Whew." He whistled with relief. "That was a close one. I hope you weren't worried."

Matilda's mouth fell open in incredulity. "Worried!" she shouted. "Leopold, you drifted out of sight on a ten-dollar raft. Of course I was worried."

The lifeguards snickered and trotted off to retrieve their punt from the shore. One of the paramedics checked Leopold's pulse and handed him a tin of lip balm, then turned to Matilda. "Take your grandfather home. Give him plenty of liquids and keep him out of the sun for at least a week."

"I'm not her grandfather." Leopold was mildly indignant.

"Not another word. Come," Matilda instructed as she grabbed Leopold's hand and tugged. (She now understood why her great-aunt had suggested she come on this trip—Leopold needed supervision.) The pair gathered their belongings from the beach and walked silently and slowly toward the house on Ocean Avenue. As they entered the yard, Leopold let out a loud whoop and declared, "Now that was one terrific adventure! Except for marrying Emma Bean, it was the best thing that's happened to me in years."

"Have you lost your mind?"

Leopold chortled. "Nope. In fact, I just found my mind. Or rather, I've had my faith restored. While I was drifting out there on the ocean, I went over *The Comprehensive Guide* in my head and I realized how much good was in it. It shouldn't be hard to fix. All it really needs is a spit polish."

Matilda dropped the deflated rafts in the yard and gave

Leopold a despairing look. "I can't believe you were thinking about your book. You could have drowned and been eaten by sharks."

Leopold smiled benevolently at his companion and patted her on the head. "Matilda, for someone so young, you fret too much. The fact is, I survived. Aside from resembling a cooked lobster, no harm befell me."

Matilda had to laugh. Leopold did look as though he'd been boiled in a vat.

Speaking of cooked lobster, that is what Marvin Jinks ordered in the fancy restaurant where he went to console himself after being hit on the head by gull droppings. He washed the buttered crustacean down with several martinis, then had a telephone brought to the table so he could call his office in New York. He was hoping to reach his administrative assistant, Bijou, but much to his immediate indigestion the call was answered by his boss. "Where are you?" Earl Slide's voice boomed in Marvin's ear. "No, forget I asked that. What kind of progress have you made with that Hillacre fellow? Hick philosophers are all the rage this year. I don't want to lose that contract."

"I, ah . . . it's d-d-down to details," Marvin stammered.

"That sounds sadly familiar."

"It's true," Marvin lied. "I've spoken to his wife and she's on our side."

"Listen, Jinks, if we lose this deal I'll personally purchase a thousand copies of the man's book and feed them to you one by one, page by page. Comprende?"

Marvin cringed. Earl Slide wasn't the type to make idle threats. "Yes sir. Have no fear. I'm on top of this deal."

Before clicking off the line, Earl Slide made a snarling noise in the phone and said, "That's exactly what I'm afraid of."

After an early supper, Holly took a shower, blow-dried her hair, put on a flower-print dress, and dabbed rouge on her already naturally rosy cheeks. She was standing in front of the bathroom mirror admiring the results of her artifice when Flea appeared in the doorway behind her and said, "You look gorgeous."

"Thank you," Holly addressed Flea's reflection in the mirror. Her relationship with Flea had improved earlier in the day when Flea showed her the poem Garland had written and sent to her by courier. Reading the poem had changed Holly's perception of Flea. Now when Holly looked at Flea, instead of seeing a chaperon who made the rules, she saw a woman excited by love. With this new image Holly was entirely empathetic. "I hope you're all right, staying in by yourself," Holly said with real concern.

Flea laughed. "I'll be fine. It's Wednesday night. I'm expecting a phone call from a man with an incurable itch."

Holly grinned and went into the living room to grab her purse. "So, I'll see you before the ten o'clock curfew."

"Rules are rules," Flea mumbled in what sounded like an apologetic tone. As Holly opened the door to leave, Flea added, "Maybe I might not notice if you're just a wee bit late."

"Thanks, Flea. That's sweet. Who knows? I might be home early. Say hey to Garland for me when he calls."

Beaufort was waiting at the tower when Holly arrived. He had his hands in his pockets, and there was a look of impatience on his face. "I was starting to wonder if I was being stood up."

"Phooey," Holly said with mock displeasure. "It's only a quarter after seven. You're the man. Did you think I was going to get here early and wait for you?"

Beaufort shrugged and let the matter pass. He withdrew his hands from his pockets and gestured toward the top of the tower. "Anyway, you're here and the line is short. You ready?"

"Ready as I'm going to be," Holly trilled.

They were alone together in the elevator, and as they rode silently upward Holly suddenly got nervous. For some reason it occurred to her that Beaufort was planning to sequester her in one of the viewing alcoves and demand an answer to the question he'd proposed earlier in the week. Holly panicked. When the door opened at the top, she informed Beaufort that she wanted to go down immediately.

Beaufort stared at Holly, assuming that she was joking, but then he saw that she was serious. "What's the matter? Are you afraid of heights?"

"That's it," Holly said quickly. "I didn't tell you before because I thought I was over it. Let's go walk through the marine park instead."

Beaufort shook his head and pushed the down button.

"I feel better already," Holly announced as they left the tower area and strolled onto a main boulevard. "Thanks for understanding."

"Hmmm," Beaufort hemmed dubiously.

"Hmmm what?" asked Holly.

"The truth is, I'm not sure I understand you."

"Why do you suppose that's so?"

"You tell me, Holly. When we met, I thought you liked me. Ever since then I've had my doubts."

Holly stopped walking and narrowed her eyes in thought. She had hoped to avoid this discussion until she was less confused about her own feelings. In spite of Beaufort's self-centered nature, she thought he was an attractive guy. He may have tended to turn caustic when he was upset, but even then he remained a gentleman and did not behave coarsely. Holly decided that she owed him the truth. "It's true, Beaufort. I liked you instantly. And I still do. But I've also had my doubts. Don't ask me what they are. I just feel them."

"Is there another guy?"

Holly blushed. She knew she had not been totally honest the first time Beaufort asked that question. "Well, there is someone who is a close friend, and he's a guy—although we're not going steady or anything."

"I knew it," Beaufort said coolly. "I wish you'd told me in the first place."

Holly felt suddenly anxious. She was more confused than ever. "I would have told you if there was anything to tell. Warren is just a friend. We aren't committed to each other. You asked me to be your girl and I've been considering saying yes. The only reason I haven't is because . . . well, I'm not ready."

"Warren, huh?"

Holly tenderly rested a hand on Beaufort's arm. "Will you be patient with me for a little while longer? This is my first time away from my family. I'm still adjusting."

Beaufort hesitated for a moment, then gestured acquiescently with his hands and said, "All right, Holly, I'll wait one more week while you think things through."

Flea flew up from the couch when Holly returned to the apartment at ten to nine.

"Sorry if I scared you," said Holly.

"That's okay. I guess I wasn't expecting you this early," Flea explained as she sat back down. "Did you have fun?"

Holly gave Flea a kind of bruised smile. "To be honest, I'm not sure. I don't think so."

"Want to talk about it?"

"Well . . . there is one thing I would like to know."

"Yes?"

Holly sat down beside Flea. "Tell me if this is normal. Once I thought I wanted something. Then, when it looked like I could have it, I wasn't sure I wanted it anymore. But every time I think I might give it up because I don't want it, I'm afraid that maybe I do. Or that I'll find out later that I did."

Flea suppressed a small smile. "I'm not a certified expert or anything, but it makes sense to me."

Holly sat thoughtfully for a moment, then reached in her purse and withdrew seven tokens, which she tossed on the table. "We didn't go on any rides. Keep those for when everyone comes to see the show this weekend. By the way, did Garland call?"

The smile that Flea had suppressed bounced back at twice its original size. "Yes, he did," she chirped happily. "And you know what, Holly? Sometimes when you think you want something, and then you get it, you find out it's exactly what you wanted all along."

Chapter Eleven

On Thursday morning Emmet telephoned Eugenna White in her office at Binkerton Town Hall. She handled the call in the same manner that she handled all calls, which was curtly and efficiently. After hearing what he wanted, she put him on hold while she checked the public calendar. When she came back on the line, she listed the summer Saturdays that the hall was available and encouraged him to reserve the one he wanted. Emmet picked August 8. It seemed like a lucky date; it was the day before his fourteenth birthday.

"I'll pencil in the eighth," Eugenna informed him, "and as soon as I receive a one-hundred-dollar security deposit— cash, check, or money order—I'll change the reservation to ink."

Emmet was shocked. "A hundred dollars! Where am I going to get a hundred dollars?"

"That's your problem," said Eugenna, sounding rather pleased with herself. "Presuming that nothing is broken, trashed, or stolen from the facility, half of your deposit will be returned within ten business days of the occupying date."

"Gripes," said Emmet after he hung up the phone.

On Friday morning Emmet and Warren arose early, got dressed in their finest clothes, gobbled a quick breakfast, and hurried from the house. Before leaving the farm, they poked their heads in the barn to see how Henry was progressing on the stilts he'd agreed to make for Warren.

"Good morning, boys," Henry said, gesturing proudly at the shellacked poles lying on a nearby sawhorse. "I still have the footrests to go, but otherwise I'm done."

"Thanks, Dad."

"I appreciate it, Mr. Dither. They look beautiful."

Henry picked up a screwdriver and asked, "Why are you two dressed like it's the first day of school?"

"Because we need a hundred dollars to reserve the Town Hall and we're going to speak with Jimmy about backing us," Emmet said as if it was the most logical explanation in the world.

"Mr. Aylor said he was behind us all the way," added Warren.

Henry's brow furrowed. "Son, I'm not sure it's proper for you to ask Jimmy to give you money."

"Not *give*, Dad. We're inviting him to *invest* in the show."

Henry expression grew more doubtful. "Emmet, a hundred dollars is a lot of money. Jimmy may feel like you're putting him on the spot."

"Actually, it's the opposite. You see, Jimmy wants us to put Alice in the show."

"Alice Aylor?" Henry said with concern.

"Yes, Alice the accordion player," Emmet confirmed. "Jimmy said she'd be mighty pleased to play in front of an audience again."

"Emmet, it's probably none of my business, but I recommend that you consider very carefully before you put Alice in your show. I've heard her play at pageants before."

"I've heard her too," Emmet declared with a laugh. "But we need the money, Dad, and sometimes you just gotta go the way the creek flows."

"Don't worry, Mr. Dither," said Warren. "We'll put Alice between acts."

When the boys arrived at the store, Jimmy was on a ladder bedecking the porch awning with red, white, and blue streamers. He was a patriotic veteran who took advantage of any opportunity to fly the flag or otherwise express his belief in the American way. Of course, he went all out for Memorial Day and the Fourth of July. Aside from hoisting the colors, Jimmy also plastered the store windows with posters of George Washington, Abe Lincoln, Ike Eisenhower, and Uncle Sam. Between the posters, the boys could see Carl on his movable chair, staring pensively out at the world.

"Howdy, boys," Jimmy said cheerfully as he tacked one end of a streamer to a post.

"Morning, Jimmy," replied Emmet. "The place looks great."

"Hello, Mr. Aylor," Warren said with polite reserve. No matter how hard he tried, he wasn't comfortable addressing Jimmy by his first name.

Jimmy descended the ladder, adjusted his pants around his waist, and gave the well-dressed boys a critical going-over. "Let me guess. You're going into politics."

"No sir," Emmet said with an embarrassed blush.

"Hmmm. Well, it's too early to go courting," Jimmy noted. "So you must want to sell me on something. Am I right?"

Emmet shrugged and look down. Warren took a sudden interest in the way the streamers were arranged.

Jimmy smiled as if he'd just drawn three aces in a poker game. "I'll be a minute finishing here; then we can go inside and parley."

Archibald left the house shortly after ten in the morning. As he was approaching the gate at the end of the driveway, he saw his brother and Warren coming home. "Where've you guys been?"

"At a business meeting," said Emmet, climbing atop the gate.

"Making deals," added Warren as he sprang up and joined Emmet. "Mr. Aylor is going to back our show."

Archibald slipped between two slats in the gate and turned. "That explains why you're dressed up like goody-goodies."

Emmet dropped down on the farm side of the gate. "Be careful what you say if you want free tickets to our show."

"Oops. Sorry," Archibald feigned repentance.

"So, Arch, why are you up so early?"

"Because I got lots of important things to do before we go to Queen's Playland tomorrow."

Emmet's expression grew suddenly somber. "I hope you're planning to visit Carl. We saw him a while ago and he looks like he needs some powerful cheering up."

"That's where I'm headed now," Archibald said glumly.

"Arch . . . is Carl sick?" asked Emmet. "He's dozing every time I see him."

Archibald blinked and looked away. He knew that Emmet cared about Carl almost as much as he did. "Carl has a lot of serious stuff on his mind. He's not dying or anything. Not yet."

Carl was asleep when Archibald arrived at the store, so Archibald spun on his heels and went to chat with Jimmy. "I hear you're bankrolling the Unlikely Trio."

"Yes. I thought it was my civic duty."

"That's *extremely* generous of you," Archibald declared. "May I have some money too?"

Although Jimmy frowned, there was a hint of amusement in his voice when he asked, "What do you need money for?"

"General purposes."

Jimmy kept a completely straight face as he explained to Archibald, "Money is funny. If I gave some to everyone who needed it for general purposes, I'd be flat broke in no time. Eventually I'd lose the store, Alice would leave me, and then I'd have to come live in your house with you."

"Our house is full," Archibald said with a sly grin. "But don't worry. I don't want your money. I was just checking to see if you still had your wits about you."

When Archibald arrived at the Hillacre estate and poked his head into the carriage house, he saw Emma Bean standing like a statue, holding a steaming cup of hot tea, staring at the brass frame of her invention. He watched for a moment before announcing his presence. "Fire," he called, just to be funny, but when his great-aunt jumped and spilled tea on her chest, he regretted his attempt at humor.

"Archibald!" Emma shouted angrily.

"I'm sorry."

After Emma's pulse rate returned to normal, she informed Archibald, "You almost gave me a heart attack."

Archibald winced regretfully. "Honestly, I'm sorry. It was dumb of me to scare you. Sometimes I forget how jumpy old people can be."

Emma rolled her eyes. She did not enjoy being referred to as an old person. Nevertheless, she let the offense pass. She had larger, more cosmic matters on her mind. She turned her attention back to the projector and began to ponder again quietly.

After a moment Archibald asked softly, "Whatcha thinking?"

"Well . . . I know that nucleic acids are held together by hydrogen bonds," Emma said without breaking her concentration. "But I'm trying to remember if all the helical phosphate ester chains in DNA are composed of carbon."

"You better look that up," suggested Archibald. "I'm not too hot on scientific details."

Emma Bean broke her train of thought and smiled. "That may be an asset, Arch. Details often obscure the big picture."

"I've always thought so."

The smile faded from Emma's face and she returned her full attention to the frame of the projector. Again she stood like a stone, and soon she began to think aloud, "The vertex is nine feet off the ground. The length of the base is nine feet. Nine times nine is eighty-one. Divided by three is twenty-seven."

"Whew," exclaimed Archibald. "What was all that about?"

"I was calculating ratios. And I may have just saved us a pound of frustration. The seat should hang twenty-*seven* inches off the ground—not twenty-*eight*, like I originally thought."

"Good work," Archibald said admiringly as he stepped forward to touch the pyramidal structure. There was much he did not know about the project (and much he didn't care to understand), but he was curious about one aspect of the endeavor: Could he use it to help Carl? "May I ask you a stupid question?"

"No."

"Sorry. May I ask you an ignorant question?"

"Yes."

Archibald hesitated, his eyes shooting upward, then down, then settling on Emma. "Is the astral plane crowded?"

"Do you mean is it full of spirits?"

"Yeah. Something like that."

Emma sighed. It was a problematic question to which there were no simple answers. "As I told you before, the astral plane is a concept. It doesn't look like anything. You can't see or touch it, really. And the spirits you're wondering about—I know you're thinking about Carl's sister—are composed of vibrations. Spirits don't have bodies. They don't take up much space. And in that sense, the answer is no—the astral plane is not crowded."

"Are you saying that Stella is just a vibration?"

"More or less. To be specific, her spirit is an aggregation of molecular vibrations held together by a strong thought. In her case, that thought is probably memory."

Archibald nodded thoughtfully. "So . . . to communicate with spirits in the astral plane, you have to speak like a vibration, and that's why you invented this machine, to send up your personal vibrations."

Emma gave Archibald a long look. She was impressed by his astuteness. "I'll be darned. You actually figured it out. Some people study the subject their whole lives and never manage to grasp the big picture."

Archibald acknowledged the compliment with a cheeky grin. "It was easy. I ignored the details."

Later that afternoon when Archibald returned to the farm, the whole house smelled like peaches. Entering through the back door, he glanced into the parlor and saw Henry and Angeline sitting on the couch. Henry waved and informed Archibald that the kitchen was off-limits. "Don't disturb your mother. She needs privacy to perform her magic."

Archibald understood. It was the day before the Fourth of July, and although the Dither clan would be going to Queen's Playland and not attending the Binkerton Independence Festival as they usually did, Clementine would be submitting several entries in the Pie and Pastry contest. "Where's Emmet and Warren?"

"In the barn," said Henry. "At least they were a while ago."

As Archibald approached the barn, he could hear Senator screeching loudly. It sounded as if the monkey was being tickled to death. Archibald hurried ahead to investigate. When he ran inside, he was astounded to see Warren standing fifteen feet in the air.

Actually, Warren wished he was doing something so stable as standing. In fact, he was tottering precariously on two slender poles. He was terribly frightened. As he was in the process of discovering, mounting the stilts had required a perch, balance, and gumption, but dismounting them required . . . well, that was what he and Emmet were currently trying to figure out.

Eventually they did solve the problem of dismounting, but not before Warren's face encountered the beam above the bay doors with a loud smack.

Chapter Twelve

At eight thirty on Saturday morning, July the Fourth, Bellamonte Smoot arrived on Dither Farm in her Pontiac Catalina. She left it idling in the driveway and went in the house to pick up the pies that Clementine was entering in the Binkerton Independence Festival culinary contest. While Bellamonte was indoors, Alice and Jimmy Aylor pulled up in Jimmy's modified '49 Ford. Behind them came Garland Barlow, carrying Acorn and Bart. Garland had just cut his engine when Millie Ross appeared in her Volkswagon Bug. Except for Bellamonte, who was going to the festival, the group was planning to travel in a convoy to Queen's Playland.

Yet no one was going anywhere until they unsnarled the traffic jam in the driveway. The group was casually discussing the best way to free their vehicles when Henry stepped into the yard and began shouting directions. It was obvious to him that Millie should reverse her Bug into the field so Jimmy could inch by Garland's truck to make room for Bellamonte's Catalina to back away from the fence, but due to the wisecracks engendered by Henry's Bermuda shorts, he had a hard time communicating his scheme. Eventually, though, the teasing subsided and Henry got the group to agree to his plan. It probably would have worked, but when Clementine appeared in the yard and suggested Henry move his truck up the hill so everyone could pull forward and turn around in the parking area, her proposal was adopted instead.

After Bellamonte drove off with Clementine's pies, a brief caucus was held, during which it was decided that Henry would lead the caravan in his '51 Chevy pickup. Clementine and Angeline would accompany him in the cab, and Archibald would ride in the back. Millie would follow behind Henry, and Acorn would ride with her. Emmet and Warren would ride with Garland, and Bart would go with Alice and Jimmy. Goosebumps and Senator were not invited.

About this same time on Saturday morning, Matilda and Leopold were kneeling in the living room of their beach house, peeking out the front window. Leopold had gone out earlier to buy more baby oil, and as he returned to the house, he'd noticed a suspicious character following him. The man was now leaning against a light pole across the street.

"Think we should call the cops?" asked Matilda.

"I don't know why," Leopold muttered softly. "He hasn't done anything threatening."

"Not yet," said Matilda. "But it's spooky the way he's just standing there. We should do something."

"I probably should have told you this earlier," Leopold said hesitantly, "but when Emma got this house for us, she hinted that it was somehow connected to a secret arm of the government. Maybe that man . . . oh, never mind. It's best not to speculate."

Matilda knew about Emma's clandestine past, and she nervously asked Leopold, "Speculate what? Do you think he's a spy? Is that it? Oh, no! What if he's got us confused with someone else? What if that man is an assassin?"

"Shush, Matilda. I told you before, you fret too much." Leopold turned on his tender knees and began crawling toward the rear of the house. "Come on, keep your head down and follow me. Let's sneak out the back door and go get some breakfast."

Matilda was aghast. "Breakfast? How can you think of food at a time like this?"

"I'm hungry," Leopold answered simply. "Now, come on. We'll eat and then stroll around in some air-conditioned stores."

Marvin Jinks continued pacing in front of the house on Ocean Avenue until noontime. By then his stomach had begun to rumble and he was ready to faint from dehydration, so he left his post and headed toward the nearest store. He was waiting in line at the register, drinking one of the two sodas he intended to purchase, when he glanced up and saw a redheaded girl and a distinctive old man with a long nose pass by on the sidewalk. He bolted after them.

Marvin got about halfway across a paved parking lot before he was tackled from behind by a man wearing a dark-blue uniform. When Marvin recovered from the shock, he shouted, "What do you think you're doing?"

The uniformed man flipped Marvin over on the pavement and yanked his arms backward. "I'm a security guard. I'm arresting you for the theft of two Big Smile sodas."

"I need to talk to those people walking down the sidewalk."

The guard turned to glance over his shoulder. He saw no one. "What people?"

"The old man and the girl. He's a famous philosopher."

"Save it for the judge," the guard replied wittily. He was a man who obviously enjoyed his job.

"No, you don't understand," Marvin pleaded. "I'm from New York. It's not the money. I'll pay for the sodas. I'll pay double if you want."

The guard snickered as he clapped a pair of handcuffs on Marvin. "You'll pay, all right. You'll pay pretty."

When the Dither party passed through the main ticket gate at Queen's Playland shortly after twelve, they were met by Holly and Flea. The group exchanged a flurry of hugs and kisses amidst a stream of strangers pouring past them into the park. Soon Flea got everyone's attention and shepherded the group to a nearby rest area where they could discuss their plans in relative peace. While Jimmy, Alice, Millie, Clementine, and Henry decided who would be responsible for whom and where they should meet if they got lost, Flea handed out passes to the three o'clock Wild West show. She also gave Archibald, Emmet, and Warren two Playland tokens apiece. (She planned to keep the extra, seventh token as a memento of her summer.)

In one of those annoying parental rulings that color the lives of all older siblings, Emmet was informed that he and Warren could roam freely—as long as they took Archibald with them. Emmet didn't bother to lodge a protest. Nor did he complain when Holly offered to give them a tour of the attractions before she was due at the arena for her first performance. (There were two Wild West shows on Saturdays and Sundays.)

"That way." Holly pointed along the central boulevard and fell into step beside Warren. "So, what happened to your face? Someone hit you with a rake?"

Warren grimaced and reached to touch the bandage on his chin. There was also a small bruise under his right eye. "Oh, this? It's just a scratch," he said modestly. "It didn't even need stitches."

Holly hemmed. "Must be a big scratch."

"A scrape, really. My face hit the top of the barn door."

Holly stopped in her tracks. "The barn door? Where did you fall from, the roof?"

"No," said Warren, turning red. "I toppled while I was walking on a pair of stilts your dad made."

Holly rolled her eyes and laughed. "Stilts, huh? I suppose you're lucky you didn't break your neck."

"Gotta do something for excitement while you're away."

"Ah, that's sweet," said Holly, and she meant it.

"So, do you like it here?"

"I love it. I've been meeting lots of fabulous people."

Although Warren tried to make the question sound casual, he was obviously pained by the mention of Holly's new friends. "Have you met anyone fabulous in particular?"

Holly pretended to think about the question. "Let me see. There's Sally Swope, our director. She's neat. And, oh yeah, my costar is pretty cool. His name is Beaufort. He rides a big roan mare named Lucy. Incidentally, there's a reception following the second show. I'll introduce him to you afterward."

"Whatever . . ." Warren replied flatly. He'd not forgotten

Holly's flip remark on the day she left the farm, and it disturbed him that she counted her costar as one of her cool new friends.

Holly saw the frown on Warren's face, but before she could lift it into a smile by changing the subject, Emmet ended their private moment with a shout. "Look. The Zing Dinger! The biggest, fastest roller coaster in North America. Come on, Warren."

"Excuse me," said Warren before hurrying to join Emmet.

Holly sighed and turned to Archibald, who was watching the scene with a distant look on his face. "You look troubled. This is an amusement park. You're supposed to be amused."

Archibald shrugged. He was thinking about Carl and he wasn't in the mood for fun.

Although Henry knew the Fourth of July was the most crowded day of the year at Queen's Playland, he was still surprised by the high number of people walking around on the same seventy-two acres of land. He hadn't been surrounded by so many strangers since his trip to New York City over a decade and a half ago. And as before, he found the experience unnerving.

Jimmy noticed Henry's agitated state, and he knew just what to do. "Pardon us," he said to Alice, Clementine, and Millie as he grabbed Henry by the arm and directed him toward the Munchen Haus restaurant. "Let's go sample a genuine Wiener schnitzel . . . maybe chase it down with one or two of those famous German beers."

Henry thought that was a brilliant proposal.

"Well, girls, it appears we've been abandoned," Alice said as the men departed. "I don't know about ya'll, but I feel compelled to drown my sorrows in yonder ice-cream parlor."

"Must have been reading my mind," Millie seconded the idea.

A happy cooing sound emanated from Angeline's stroller.

Clementine smiled agreeably and pushed the stroller forward. As her group entered the parlor, she mused aloud, "I wonder what Flea and Garland are up to."

"I don't dare imagine," replied Alice.

Millie began to giggle. "I do."

An hour later, as Jimmy and Henry left the Munchen Haus, they heard an announcement over a loudspeaker that the porpoises would be fed in five minutes. The public was invited to the marine park to witness the event. Jimmy glanced at his watch. "Holly's show doesn't start for another hour. Want to see porpoises eat?"

"Sure, I'll watch that," Henry agreed with a burp. "I've never seen a porpoise before. Jimmy, you lead the way."

Jimmy hailed a Glee Guide and was directed down a winding path. Moments later, when he and Henry arrived at the artifical lagoon, the viewing stands were nearly full. Fortunately, Jimmy spied an empty gap near the top of the bleachers and scrambled up to secure seats. Henry followed, and after they were settled, Jimmy nudged him with an elbow. "I see some of our gang."

"Where?" asked Henry. All he saw was a sea of faces.

"There." Jimmy pointed to the north end of the concrete pond. "Near the platform. That's Archibald standing with Acorn and Bart. Emmet and Warren are right behind them."

Henry nodded, then hiccuped. "Now I SEE thEM."

Soon a young man in a white uniform approached the platform and addressed the crowd through a small microphone attached to his shirt. He spoke of how smart porpoises were, bragged a bit about how well Queen's Playland provided for the three specimens living in the lagoon, then pointed to the arrangement of hoops suspended over the water. "The porpoise of these hoops," said the attendant, pausing as the audience groaned at his pitiful pun, "is to demonstrate the athleticism and power of adult, blunt-snouted *Phocaena*." The attendant pulled a large mullet from a bucket and signaled for one of his colleagues to open a submerged gate. Suddenly the water in the lagoon rippled with movement, and then a sleek gray mammal broke from the surface and sailed through one of the hoops. The attendant walked to the end of the platform, held the fish up by its tail, and whistled. The porpoise shot through another hoop, approached the platform, and rose up in the water. The man dropped the fish, which promptly disappeared down the porpoise's throat. After waiting for the applause to subside, he announced, "Now I need a volunteer."

Many of the youngsters in the audience cried out and waved their hands above their heads. The attendant swung his gaze over the crowd until his eye settled fatefully on Archibald. Perhaps it was the bored look on Archibald's face that caught the man's attention. Or maybe it was Acorn, gesturing wildly at Archibald's head. At any rate, the man motioned for Archibald to join him on the platform. Archibald shrugged nonchalantly and obliged. As he approached the end of the platform, he could hear Emmet urging him to do the chicken dance.

From his seat high above the lagoon, Henry Dither cringed. He could hear Emmet as well. Fortunately, Archibald ignored his brother's rebellious request. He wasn't in the mood for chicken dancing. Even so, what happened next was almost as funny as the chicken dance. It was certainly as memorable.

First the attendant interviewed Archibald and introduced him to the crowd. He might have been a nice man, but he had no talent for humor. After several of his jokes fell flat (he told the same ones every day, all summer), he fished another mullet from the bucket and led Archibald to the pool side of the platform. The man pantomimed instructions on how to hold the fish over the water and when to drop it, then whistled shrilly.

Two seconds later a porpoise shot out of the water and soared for the fish. Archibald was startled. He reacted by dropping the mullet and pitching forcefully backward. In doing so his left elbow jabbed the attendant in the groin. The man crumpled, and knocked Archibald in the opposite direction.

Archibald stumbled and fell from the platform. There should have been a splash when he hit the water, but there was hardly a smack. Much to the dazzlement of Archibald and everyone watching, Archibald's descent ceased an inch above the surface. His knees were bent to his chest, his arms were stuck forward, and the small of his back was resting on the broad snout of a playful porpoise. With a whoosh, Archibald zoomed across the water.

As Archibald made a circuit around the lagoon the crowd erupted in a roar of laughter.

Then—as if the scene was not astonishing enough—Archibald zipped down the center of the lagoon, flew up in the air, and shot cleanly through the highest hoop. And yet again, when everyone expected a splash, there was no splash. With the deft agility of a trained seal catching a beach ball, the playful porpoise swam swiftly forward, elevated its head above the water and presented Archibald with a seat.

Some members of the audience were laughing so hard they fell on the pavement, others had tears in their eyes and could not speak, yet no one was more tickled than Jimmy Aylor. Although he'd seen Archibald perform the chicken dance in the Binkerton Independence Festival parade—and that had been hilarious—he was much more amused now than then. He embraced Henry for support and declared, "That boy of yours has a knack for shining on the Fourth of July."

Henry did not reply. The combined effects of the Munchen Haus and the sight of his son traveling round and round the lagoon caused his head to start spinning. It continued to spin even after the porpoise delivered Archibald safely back to the platform and the collapsed attendant.

Chapter Thirteen

Show business is an erratic affair. Seasoned entertainers know that some shows go smoothly while, for no apparent reason, other shows bump along like flat tires. A performer can do a thing on one day and have a success, then do the exact same thing on the next and have a flop. Do these erratic results reflect the unique chemistry of different audiences, or is the outcome of each show dependent on the whim of some thespian god? No one really knows.

On this Fourth of July the three o'clock Wild West show at Queen's Playland was a tremendous success. In a way that had never happened before and was unlikely to happen again, each member of the cast was absorbed in the movement of the spectacle and the audience was witness to a kind of magical illusion. The cowboys were real cowboys, the Indians were true natives of the land, and the pioneers were a people in search of a home.

To the discerning critic or the casual observer, one fact was indisputable: Holly Dither and her pony Dan were the source of the show's power. The quick darts, the pinpoint turns, her lighter-than-air manner in the saddle . . . it was all a seductive prelude to her acrobatic side-switching, daring handstands, and back-roll dismount.

Henry was so proud of the applause accorded his daughter, he threw back his head and hollered, "Every one of my kids is special. You should hear the youngest girl sing."

Henry's words were hardly out of his mouth when an elbow jabbed him in the ribs. He turned to Clementine, who berated him in an angry whisper, "You can make a fool of yourself if you insist, but don't embarrass the whole family."

"No one heard me," Henry said defensively.

"I did," Clementine retorted with a sobering look.

Henry winced sheepishly, then raised his hands and began to clap.

There was a reception in the Royal Pavillion following the afternoon show. As the room filled with performers and their families, friends, and chaperons, Holly was surrounded and swamped with so many compliments she could barely acknowledge them all. Even for her, the attention was overwhelming. She blushed and blew kisses to her mom and dad, then graciously attempted to share the glory with the rest of the crew. "Much of the credit belongs to our director, who made it all happen, and to my wonderful supporting cast," Holly modestly informed her fans. "Without them I would have been just another trick rider making a scene."

As Holly stood in the center of the room soaking up the attention, Beaufort stood alone in a corner. He was fuming. In his mind it was clear that Holly had used unfair tactics to grab the spotlight, and he wasn't the least bit mollified by her attempts at modesty. If she's so humble, he reasoned darkly, she never would have sprung an unscripted handstand during the rescue scene.

Later, as the reception wound down and the guests were beginning to leave, Holly grabbed Warren by the hand and dragged him toward the corner where Beaufort had parked himself. Warren offered a feeble protest, explaining that he and Emmet had planned to ride the Gravity Bender. Holly refused to let go. "The Gravity Bender will wait," she informed Warren before calling across the room to Emmet, "Take Acorn and Bart with you. Warren is busy here for the next little while. We'll catch up."

When Warren offered some light resistance, Holly increased the pressure on his hand and pulled him across the room.

Holly had noticed earlier that Beaufort was sulking, but it was not until she and Warren arrived in his corner that she saw how upset he was. But it was too late to retreat, so Holly simply ignored his angry glare and said politely, "Beaufort, I'd like you to meet my friend Warren Robinson. He was born up in New Hampshire, but he lives in Virginia now." She paused, gestured from one boy to the other and continued, "Warren, this is my costar, Beaufort B. Beaumont. He hails from down near Halifax, Virginia."

"How do you do?" said Warren, extending the hand that Holly had finally released.

Beaufort surveyed Warren with a supercilious look, then lifted his right hand and allowed it to be shaken.

"I thought you were good in the show," said Warren.

"Hmph."

Warren figured he'd try once more to be friendly. "That was a nice-looking mare you were riding."

"Most Thoroughbreds are."

Holly could hardly believe what was happening. This was no way to treat a friend of hers; especially one who was behaving so decently. Suddenly it was out with Holly the diplomat and in with Holly the Hun. "All right, Beaufort. What's wrong with you?"

"*You're* asking *me?*" Beaufort said in mock surprise.

"Yes, I'm asking you," Holly snapped.

If there was ever a moment when Holly had been intimidated by her costar, it was now a part of history. She showed no sign of weakness when Beaufort engaged her in an eye-to-eye showdown. As the tension continued to mount, Warren decided he would rather be elsewhere. "You two talk. I'm going to see if I can catch Emmet," Warren said quickly to Holly, adding as he turned, "Have a happy day, Beaufort."

"Warren, don't rush off," pleaded Holly.

"Isn't that like a bruised and bandaged Yankee?" Beaufort chortled. "When there's heat, they run."

Warren stopped quicker than you could say halt. He drew an even breath, turned slowly, and walked straight at Beaufort. When there was less than six inches between them, Warren stopped for a second time. He was generally a peaceful guy and he did not get riled easily. Still, he was not a wimp; he knew what he approved of and what he disliked. He studied Beaufort until the older boy blinked, then smiled as if he'd been amused by a kitten. "For the record, Beaufort B. Whatever-your-name-is. I'm not leaving because of the heat. I'm leaving because of a bad smell. Holly is fine. She reminds me of roses. I think it's you that stinks."

Beaufort flinched and stepped back before he could stop himself. As he was struggling to think of a rejoinder, Warren walked slowly away. "Goodness, Holly," Beaufort said haughtily. "You sure do have some touchy friends."

Suddenly Holly could not imagine why she had ever been attracted to Beaufort. She watched as Warren left the pavillion, and when the door closed behind him, another one opened in her heart. She realized now that Warren was the guy for her. She spun to face Beaufort. "We have to work together for the rest of the summer, so I won't tell you how rude I think you are. But I will say this—" Holly paused, and then, in the biggest insult she could think of, she shook a finger at Beaufort and said, "The Beaumonts have a long way to go before I ever think highly of them again."

Beaufort's eyes bulged with bewilderment, and the superior chip on his shoulder plummeted to the floor. "I didn't mean to hurt his feelings. I was just—"

"Being a creep," Holly finished Beaufort's sentence for him, before spinning around and leaving the pavillion.

Holly arrived at the Gravity Bender just as Warren took Acorn's place beside Emmet near the front of a long line. She called to Warren, and he waved to her, but then the line surged forward and he passed from view.

As Acorn walked into the open, Holly scowled at him and asked, "Why'd you let Warren do that?"

"Why'd I let Warren do what?" Acorn asked anxiously.

"Take your place in line," Holly snapped.

Acorn felt somewhat relieved. He could answer that question. "I let Warren take my place because he asked nicely."

Holly frowned and shook her head. "Men. You're all the same. Completely insensitive to a woman's needs."

Acorn's mouth dropped open. He was as rattled as a baffle in a worn-out muffler.

Except for a strange incident involving the double Ferris wheel and one of Angeline's diapers, the rest of the afternoon passed pleasantly and smoothly for the visitors from Willow County. By prior arrangement, the group met by the Eiffel Tower at six that evening.

While Jimmy and Henry discussed whether they should stay and see the fireworks or leave before the holiday traffic got heavy, Alice, Clementine, and Millie joked whether Flea had kidnapped Garland or Garland had kidnapped Flea. Alice held her sides and laughed when she spotted the pair approaching from a distance. "Hold on. There's Romeo and Juliet now."

Millie and Clementine followed Alice's gaze and saw the couple walking hand in hand. Although they were too far away to hear what was being said, they were obviously exchanging tender sentiments. Flea was blushing with a kind of neon happiness, and Garland marched along as though he had springs in his shoes.

"They look so happy," observed Alice.

Clementine thought they looked a lot more than merely happy, but she did not attempt to express the notion. She just smiled and watched as the couple approached. When Flea joined the group, the women aimed inquiring looks at her and waited for her to speak. But Flea was not forthcoming. She grinned cryptically, dropped into a squat by the stroller, and chirped baby talk at Angeline.

Garland inserted himself between Henry and Jimmy. When they asked his opinion about staying for the fireworks, he shrugged and said, "Whatever you fellows say."

Meanwhile, off to the side, Holly was attempting to share a private moment with Warren. She was hampered by the presence of Emmet and Archibald, but not defeated. She sidled as close to Warren as possible and whispered, "I hope you'll kindly forgive me."

"For what?" Warren asked innocently.

Holly moaned, smiled quickly, then moaned again. "For being wishy-washy about us. I didn't actually do anything wrong, but I *was* tempted."

Warren looked down and shuffled his feet.

Holly usually found Warren easy to read, but at this moment she could not determine what he was feeling. Her worst fear, of course, was that he wasn't feeling much at all. "Listen," she said softly. "I have lots to say to you, but this isn't the best time to talk. If it's okay, I'm going to write you a letter."

Warren, in spite of everything, still felt quite tender toward Holly. "Sure," he said with a deferential nod. "You can write me a letter."

Somewhat to Henry's surprise, no one complained when he announced that the party would not be staying for the fireworks. At the least he'd expected an argument from Archibald, but his youngest son accepted the news calmly. Indeed, Archibald seemed gladdened by the decision. He's probably still in shock from his experience in the marine park, thought Henry.

The truth was, except for Angeline, everyone was pooped.

Chapter Fourteen

The next morning, back on Dither Farm, Archibald sat on the front porch bemoaning his mother's decree that people should not visit their neighbors before twelve thirty on Sundays. He had argued with Clementine on numerous occasions, trying to get her to lift the edict, but she had refused to budge on the matter.

So Archibald waited until twelve twenty-nine before leaving the farm. When he arrived at Aylor's Store, which opened at one on Sundays, he proceeded to the back of the building and rapped on Carl's bedroom window. There was no response. He rapped again, and after a moment he heard bedsprings creaking. Then he heard floorboards doing the same. A shadow approached the window, the curtains were pulled aside, and Carl's big face appeared behind the dingy glass. "I'm not in the mood for company."

"I'm not company. I'm your pal."

Carl stood silently for a moment without moving.

"Open up, or I'll blow your house down."

Carl shook his head, shrugged in a resigned manner, and went to the back door. He greeted Archibald with an unwelcoming look, then ambled back into his bedroom.

Archibald knew the big guy was hurting and was not offended by the inhospitable reception. He followed Carl into his cramped quarters, sat on the trunk at the foot of Carl's rumpled bed, and asked, "Want to hear how it went yesterday?"

Carl grunted ambivalently. Archibald interpreted the sound as a yes and began recounting the trip to Queen's Playland. He boasted about Dan and Holly's performance in the Wild West show, mentioned that he'd seen Flea and Garland holding hands, then got off the trunk and demonstrated the way Emmet had walked after riding the Gravity Bender. Carl watched impassively. He remained stone-faced until Archibald told him about the incident in the marine park. At that, Carl cracked a rusty smile. The image of Archibald zipping across the top of the water while the crowd roared with laughter was too amusing to ignore. "That must have taken you by surprise," Carl observed with a chuckle. "Sometimes I used to see porpoises from the ship. They're amazing creatures. Intelligent, and friendly, too."

After so many weeks of nothing but misery, the sound of Carl chuckling was like candy to Archibald. "The porpoise that caught me seemed like a really nice animal. I could tell he was trying to keep me dry. I never felt like I was in danger."

"You weren't frightened?"

"I might have been a little scared," Archibald admitted.

Carl crossed his arms and sighed. It would be stretching the truth to say he was happy at this moment, but it did seem as if he was somewhat relieved of his crushing depression.

Archibald was heartened by the turn in Carl's mood, and he wanted to do whatever he could to sustain the improvement. As of yet, he had not told Carl about Emma Bean's invention. This wasn't because he'd given Emma Bean his word that he'd keep the Projector a secret; it was because he didn't want Carl to develop any unrealistic expectations. Still, he wanted to signal that hope might be on the horizon. "So . . ." Archibald smiled knowingly. "I can't tell you what, but I've got something cooking, and if it comes out right, it may help us get to Stella."

The announcement put an immediate end to Carl's easy mood. "Get to Stella? What do you mean?"

"I mean there might be a way we can contact Stella and ask about the promise you made."

"How?"

"That's confidential. You'll just have to trust me."

"I've always trusted you, Arch, but Stella has been gone for a long time. It's hardly possible for you to contact her."

"I'm going to try. I know it won't be easy."

Carl peered questioningly at Archibald for a moment; then his expression shifted to a look of doubt, and he said in a weary voice, "Does this have something to do with Emma Bean's secret project that you hinted to me about?"

"Maybe. Maybe not," Archibald mumbled softly.

"You're not going to do anything risky, are you?"

"Who, me?" Archibald said with an abashed look. "Safety is my new middle name."

As Archibald was leaving from the rear of the building, he encountered Jimmy Aylor, who was on his way from the house to the store. Jimmy saluted Archibald and smiled. "Heck of a show you put on yesterday. Funniest thing I've ever seen."

"Glad you enjoyed it."

Jimmy glanced at the window in back of the store, and his manner shifted from glib to grave. "You were visiting Carl. How's he doing?"

Archibald exhaled loudly. "He's more or less the same as he's been all summer. Maybe a little better."

Jimmy nodded thoughtfully. "Carl is slow sometimes, but in the long run he's a winner. I don't know how or when, but I bet he'll come around eventually."

"I expect you're right," Archibald agreed.

A faraway look entered Jimmy's eyes, and he stood frozen for a moment without speaking. Then he rested a hand on Archibald's shoulder and began musing aloud. "I remember sometimes after a big battle Carl would withdraw into himself and not speak to anybody on the ship for two or three weeks at a spell. From the admiral to the cook, we'd all worry about him, but there was nothing we could do. Time would pass . . . and then one day we'd hear singing in the shower and we knew he was right again."

"I didn't know Carl could sing. I've never heard him."

"Oh yeah," said Jimmy. "Carl has a beautiful voice. Big as a bull and smooth as silk."

At one o'clock on Sunday, while the rest of the family were somewhere outdoors, Emmet stood motionlessly in the hallway between the parlor and the kitchen. It wasn't hot in the house, but he was sweating as he warily eyed the telephone on the hall table. After studying the intrument for several tense minutes, he snatched up the receiver and dialed PKY-5595.

He could hear the mechanical sound of a phone ringing in King County. It rang and rang, and rang again. "Baptists," Emmet swore under his breath. "They stay at church forever on Sundays."

Emmet heard a click, then a man saying hello.

"Co-con-contessa, please," Emmet stammered.

"Who may I say is calling?"

"Emmet Dither."

"Hey, Emmet. It's Mike Cunningham, Contessa's dad. How have you been getting along?"

"I'm fine. Thank you."

"And how's your monkey?"

"Senator is fine."

"Good. Glad to hear it," Mike said cheerfully. "Hold on, I'll get Contessa."

While Emmet waited for Contessa to come to the phone, one of his immediate fears was realized: Henry strolled into the house, saw him sweating nervously, and quipped, "Who are you calling, the President?"

"No, Dad," Emmet said quickly.

Henry pointed at the phone. "A girl?"

Just as Emmet was answering his father with an embarrassed nod, Contessa said hello. "Hi. Hold on a second," he said into the receiver, gesturing frantically for his father to move on.

"Excuse me," Henry mumbled as he started toward the kitchen. He was proud of his kids. He really was.

Emmet returned the receiver to his mouth. "Sorry about that, Contessa. I had a problem, but it's gone now. So, how are you?"

"Fine. Yourself?"

"Great. I've got good news. Guess what."

"What?"

"We got an investor for the show and have the Town Hall reserved for August eighth."

"That's wonderful," Contessa trilled.

"Yeah. So, the investor says we should charge five dollars a ticket. Do you think that's too much?"

"Of course not. It's a bargain."

"I hope you're right," Emmet said with guarded cheerfulness. He was beginning to worry about whether he had enough decent material lined up for the show. "So . . . if you're still interested, maybe we should get together and feel things out."

"Excuse me, Emmet," Contessa said in a suddenly cool tone. "What exactly are you trying to say?"

Emmet blushed, thankful that Contessa could not see over the phone. "You know, rehearse and go over details. Plan the poster and stuff."

"Oh, yes," Contessa said with a relieved giggle. "That's very professional. When do you suggest we meet?"

"Anytime. The sooner the better, for me."

"Okay. Let me go talk to Dad. Maybe he can give me a ride tomorrow. Are you busy right now?"

"No. Just talking to you, that's all."

"Then don't go anywhere for a while. I'll call you back."

"Right-o," said Emmet. He didn't mind waiting at all.

Five minutes later when the phone rang, Emmet grabbed it and answered in a deeper-than-normal voice, "Dither residence. This is Emmet speaking."

"Hi, Emmet. It's Bellamonte. Is Clementine there?"

"She's outside. May I take a message?"

"Yes. Tell your mother that her peach pie was awarded a blue ribbon and her cherry pie got an honorable mention."

"Okay, I'll tell her."

"So, how was the trip to Queen's Playland?"

Emmet cringed. Bellamonte Smoot was a famous talker, and he was afraid she might cause him to miss Contessa's call. "Queen's Playland was a blast. Lots of fun. I'll tell Mom you called. Take care, Bellamonte. Bye now."

Emmet hung up the phone and sat back down to wait. He didn't know it, but he was about to learn a lesson (it would be one of many) about the way some girls keep appointments. Although Contessa had implied that she'd call him right back, the phone would not ring again for another two hours.

Archibald walked slowly and ponderously down the shaded center of Campbell's Creek Road, but when he reached the little bridge by Weeping Willow Swamp and saw the Hillacre house on the hill, he picked up his pace. It was possible, he thought, that Emma had completed the Projector while he was away, and the prospect of activating her invention made the amusement-park offerings look like baby toys by comparison.

He went directly to the carriage house and peeked through a crack in the closed doors. A ray of sunshine poured through the skylight and caused the piezoelectric crystal atop the brass frame to sparkle brightly. Emma was sitting in the lotus position on the floor. Archibald initially thought that she was staring at the crystal, but when he tiptoed forward, he saw that her eyes were closed. Her forearms rested upon her knees and she was making zeros with her thumbs and forefingers.

Archibald uttered her name softly. There was no response. He raised his voice slightly, "Oh, Aunt Emma."

Still no movement.

Archibald could not resist the temptation that now flew into his mind: "There's a snake beside you."

Emma Bean whirled around faster than a lizard after a fly. "You'd better not be joking."

Archibald hemmed, hawed, then hemmed again. "I'm terribly sorry," he said meekly. "I've been trying to get your attention for the last fifteen minutes."

"No you haven't," Emma said with a smirk as she rose to her feet. "I heard you when you came in."

Archibald reddened and turned to study the Projector. At a glance it appeared more complete than when he'd last seen it. "Wow. Look at that. It's beautiful. Gosh, Aunt Emma, I didn't expect it to be so pretty. So . . . is it ready? Have you tried it?"

Emma rued the day she had taken Archibald on as a partner. She wanted to scream, but instead she groaned and said, "Yes to your first question. I mounted the crystal this morning. *No* to your second. I haven't had a chance to try it. I was gearing up for that when you broke my concentration."

"Gearing up?"

Emma took a deep breath and explained, "I was meditating. Remember I told you that the Projector works on vibrations?"

Archibald nodded.

"Well, when I was meditating—emphasis on the *was*—I was clearing the clutter from my mind and modulating my brain waves. The Astral Projector is a refined resonating instrument. It must be played delicately."

Archibald shifted uneasily. "I don't get it."

"Try thinking of the Projector as a radio that plays mental frequencies. Then consider that different states of mind generate different vibrational frequencies. To successfully project into the astral plane, you must be in a mobile, transitional mode of consciousness, like in the morning when you awake from a dream. I was using meditation to enter that state of mind."

Archibald jutted his bottom lip forward and rubbed his chin. "Hmm. I might understand what you're trying to say. Okay if I give it a whirl?"

Emma frowned. "It's not a toy to be played with lightly, Archibald. You don't just give it a whirl. You think long and hard about what you're doing and prepare yourself before you attempt to activate the Projector."

Archibald sighed with disappointment and looked down. There was a pebble on the floor. He picked it up with his toes and tossed it aside. "I can take a hint. It's your invention. You paid for the parts and did most of the work. I'll wait my turn. You should definitely go first."

Emma laughed. In spite of Archibald's unsubtle style, she was tickled by his enduring gumption. "I will, later, when I'm all alone."

Archibald did not laugh, yet he did grin slyly as he lifted his gaze and announced, "I guess I'll be going now."

Matilda and Leopold stood on the beach on Sunday evening and watched as the light faded over the ocean. A day and a half had passed since they'd seen the strange man loitering on the street across from the house, and they no longer felt threatened. To the contrary, they were both immensely relaxed. Leopold's sunburn had diminished to the point where his clothes quit hurting, and he was enjoying a renewed sense of personal purpose. His mishap on the raft—or, as he phrased it, his brisk dance with mortality—had stimulated his intellect and heightened his appreciation of life. *Lucky to breathe* was his new motto. Now all he wanted to do was return to his Inner Sanctum and resume work on *The Comprehensive Guide*. Matilda was happy because Leopold was happy, and because they would be going home the next day. She missed her bed and she missed Goosebumps. In that order.

Chapter Fifteen

Henry was waiting at the station in Bricksburg on Monday afternoon when Matilda and Leopold got off the bus. As he threw his arms around Matilda, he asked Leopold, "What happened to you?"

"Overexposure," Leopold said in a clipped tone. He was not interested in discussing his sunburn.

"He fell asleep on a raft," Matilda explained, adding with a laugh, "the current was sweeping him toward Europe when the lifeguards caught up."

"Oh," said Henry. "I hear Europe is nice this time of year."

Leopold wasn't humored. He groaned and threw his bags in the back of the truck.

"So, Dad, how was Holly's show?"

"Amazing. Holly was great. And you'll never believe what happened to Archibald at the marine park. Crazy kid. Hop in. I'll tell you all about it on the way home."

As Henry drove westward into the familiar heart of Willow County, Leopold stuck his head out the window and let the wind tousle his hair. (A puff would have sufficed to tangle the thin tuft on his head.) Leopold was getting excited about seeing his wife again after a week apart. Although they were an unusually independent couple who related more like a team than as a loving pair, they were united in wedlock and bound to each other with mutual admiration. Leopold was surprised by how much he missed her. "So . . . ah, Henry. Any idea how Emma is doing?"

"She's fine, I believe," said Henry. "At least I haven't heard otherwise."

Moments later when Henry dropped Leopold in his yard, the carriage-house doors were shut and Leopold correctly presumed that Emma was inside working. He felt a twinge of disappointment that she didn't drop what she was doing and rush out to welcome him home, but he wasn't upset. He gave Matilda a kiss on her forehead, thanked Henry for the ride, and wandered into the house. He knew that inventors, like philosophers, walked a thin line and were easily disturbed.

Leopold dropped his bags in the kitchen and went directly to the Inner Sanctum. Emma would find him when she was ready.

Sure enough, about an hour later, Emma found Leopold sitting in the swivel chair at his worktable. "Hi, handsome," she said as she entered the Sanctum.

Leopold welcomed her with a wink.

Emma halted on her way across the room. "You need to put aloe vera on your face right away. I have some in the kitchen. I'll go get it."

"Don't go. My old face will keep for a few minutes," said

Leopold, beckoning Emma forward. "Besides, what it needs right now is a kiss."

Emma smiled and resumed her approach. It made her happy to see that Leopold missed her. During the past few days she had suffered from a series of failed attempts to activate the Astral Projector, and she was ripe for some old-fashioned comfort. She sat on the arm of Leopold's chair and gave him a gentle peck on his cheek. When he extended his arm around her, she giggled and fell sideways into his lap. "So, how did your getaway go?" she asked.

"In a word, super," said Leopold. Then he praised Matilda for behaving like a lady, remarked on the latest swimwear fashions, and casually mentioned his adventure at sea. Almost as an afterthought, he told Emma about the suspicious man that had been watching the house.

Emma asked Leopold to describe the man. When he did, she chuckled. "That was a literary agent. He came here looking for you one day and I fed him some tale about you being a guest of a rival agency. I confess, I told him that you were in Virginia Beach, in a house on Ocean Avenue, but I never imagined he'd actually find you."

"He got close, but he didn't find me," Leopold noted, then mused under his breath, "wonder what ever became of the fellow."

(Although Leopold had no way of knowing so, Marvin Jinks was still immersed in the ugly sequence of events that began when the security guard ambushed him in the convenience-store parking lot. Before the nightmare was over, Marvin would spend three nights in jail and pay a fine of four hundred dollars. It would cost him two hundred dollars retrieving his car, which had been impounded off the street, and he would have to shell out an additional three hundred clearing his hotel bill. And all of this would occur before he started the drive back to Manhattan. Along the way he would get a speeding ticket in Maryland and a flat tire in Delaware.)

Leopold quickly forgot about the agent and asked Emma how it was going with her invention. She sighed dolorously and told him, "Terrible. It doesn't work."

"Not at all?"

"Nothing. Not even a tingle."

As Leopold rubbed his hand affectionately over Emma's back, his eyes rested on the flap-winged flying machine that hung from the ceiling of the room. It was a model of a Leonardo da Vinci drawing, and he kept it for inspirational purposes. After a moment he hemmed philosophically and advised Emma, "Don't take it to heart. To begin with, you were reaching beyond the grasp of most people. When you aim that high, you can't expect to succeed with every shot."

"Platitudes won't help," replied Emma, adding glibly, "Maybe I can sell it as art. Archibald thinks it's beautiful."

Leopold ignored Emma's defeatist humor. For some reason he'd suddenly recalled the rare engsi carpet that Emma had hidden under the stairwell. It was a tribal weaving with proven magical properties, and he seemed to remember that its power was somehow connected to the phases of the moon. "Perhaps your invention is subject to certain external and invisible influences."

"Such as . . . ?" said Emma.

"Well . . . your measurements may be accurate and the numbers may add up, but there's always that extra dimension when dealing with the parametaphysical sciences. It's only a hunch, but maybe the Projector needs a cosmic booster."

"Explain."

"I can't really," Leopold conceded. "But I was thinking of your rug and wondering if maybe the Astral Projector needed some lunar grease. You know, the right sidereal alignment."

"I'd thought of that," said Emma as she snuggled against Leopold's chest. "I plan to try it again during the next full moon. That's on the twenty-fifth of July."

A silence ensued, until Leopold yawned and said, "I think I'll go up and take a little nap."

Emma made a small sound in her throat and moved to rise from his lap. "I'll come along and fluff your pillows."

Leopold smiled contentedly. It was good to be home.

Later that afternoon, following yet another successful Wild West show, Holly was in the climate-controlled barn giving Dan his daily rubdown when Beaufort approached the paddock and leaned over the railing. Holly continued to brush Dan's withers and did not look up until several seconds after Beaufort said hello. He was not put off by her manner. He'd been expecting a chilly reception. "Don't worry," he said quickly. "I'm not going to ask for forgiveness. However, I have come to make amends."

"How civilized," Holly muttered, dropping to a knee and drawing the brush over Dan's right foreleg. As far as she was concerned, Beaufort had shown his true colors and they definitely did not harmonize with her Willow County hues. In short, she was no longer charmed by or interested in his personal complexities. Besides, that morning she'd seen him flirting with a saucy-eyed pioneer named Sarah Fenning.

Beaufort knew he had behaved like an ass and he was willing

to accept the consequences. "Listen, Holly. It was wrong the way I treated Warren. I admit it. Accept my apology."

Holly stopped brushing Dan and raised her eyes. "Thanks for admitting that you were wrong, because you were. I accept your apology."

"So, do we have a trucc?" asked Beaufort. "Can we still be friends?"

Holly paused to weigh the question, then smiled thinly and told Beaufort, "Let's start with a truce and see how that goes."

An hour later Holly returned to the apartment just as Flea was putting dinner on the table. Not just any dinner—it was Holly's favorite meal: fried chicken, green beans, corn bread, mashed potatoes, and iced tea.

Flea said grace and they began to eat. Several nourishing moments passed; then Holly dabbed her mouth with a napkin and said, "There's something I want to tell you."

Flea's mouth was full, so she nodded.

"Mostly I just wanted to thank you for being so nice," Holly began. "I know I hogged Warren yesterday when everyone was saying good-bye. You hardly got the chance to speak with him. It wasn't fair of me. I mean, you're his mom now and everything."

Flea swallowed and replied, "It looked as if the two of you were having a private discussion."

"It was private, but it wasn't much of a discussion. I did most of the talking. Anyway, thanks for not interrupting us."

"You're welcome. I know how difficult it is saying good-bye to someone you know you're going to miss."

All of a sudden Holly felt a deep emotional stirring. Then, surprising both herself and Flea with her frank honesty, she blurted, "Flea, I'm afraid I love Warren as much as Garland loves you."

"That's nothing to be afraid of," replied Flea, adding with a giggle. "Not unless you intend to start writing poems."

Holly grinned. "Not me. Although I do have a very persuasive letter to compose."

The previous several weeks had been abnormally busy for many individuals from Willow County, but as of Tuesday, July 7, life resumed its normal pace. Now that the dog days of summer loomed ahead on the calendar, most Willowites slipped back into a time-filled groove where mellow was the theme of each day. This was in accordance with tradition, of course, as well as a response to the searing heat and steaming humidity that suddenly gripped the county.

Matilda was content spending her time alone in her gloriously quiet bedroom with her books. She aimed to enjoy every free minute of solitude before Holly returned at the end of August.

Aside from catering to Angeline, Clementine dedicated the ensuing weeks to organizing her business accounts and ordering container labels for the fall cider season. After those things were settled, she spent the shady part of each day fussing with weeds in her garden.

Oddly, it was Henry who broke with routine. He did so by teaming up with Wade Butcher on a contract to disassemble and move a barn from Binkerton to King County. Thus he spent most of his days away from the farm. (There was no need to worry about Henry working in the heat. As anyone who had ever partnered a job with Wade Butcher would attest, the man pursued his ambitions at a turtle's tempo.)

Warren settled into an easy routine. Basically he had only two priorities. The first was not to tumble from the stilts and reinjure his bruised chin. The second was to check the mailbox three times a day.

After letting Archibald try the Astral Projector on two occasions, Emma Bean formally limited the number of hours he was welcome at the estate to one a week. She used the excuse that Leopold needed time to recover from his vacation. Archibald wasn't fooled. He knew she was frustrated with the Projector and wanted to work on it alone, but he really didn't care what she did. He was busy being discontent. As a matter of honor, he'd decided not to be happy again until Carl Plummers found a way out of the bog where he was mired.

During this hot period Leopold sat down in the Inner Sanctum and replied to all the agents and publishers who had sent him letters. "Sorry," he wrote, "but *The Comprehensive Guide* is not quite ready for public consumption. I appreciate the interest and will contact you when the manuscript is complete. Regards, L. W. Hillacre." After the replies were posted, he buckled down and started fine-tuning his book.

And then there was Emmet, as apprehensive as a long-tailed cat in a rocking-chair factory. Not only did he have a big show to sweat—a show for which he had no singer and barely enough material to fill an hour—but on three separate, disappointing occasions Contessa Cunningham had called at the last minute to postpone her visit.

Part Three

Chapter Sixteen

It was four in the morning. The world was as still as a rock, and stone quiet. The late-July moon, three Earth rotations away from full, had just set. As it left the sky, it stole the last licks of silvery light from the treetops around Aylor's Store. The forests and fields were now draped in darkness. It had been a splendid night for owls. All small varmints that valued their lives were nestled deep in burrows or hidden in the hearts of haystacks.

Carl wore boxer shorts and a T-shirt. He was on his back with a sheet pulled over him. As he slept, a colorful montage of fleeting images danced lightly across the wrinkled roof of his mind. His internal systems operated on automatic pilot.

Out of nowhere Carl heard Stella saying, "My strength is fading. This will be my final visit."

Carl's face twitched, his lips smacked dryly together, and he floated slowly to the surface of his dreams. As he struggled to open his eyes, Stella's voice whispered inside him like a breeze stirring from a fire. "It was a simple promise, made for you. You must remember to keep it."

"Stella." Carl awoke at the sound of his own voice and sat up in the darkness. He tore the sweaty sheet off the bed and threw it across the room. Already he could sense that Stella was gone. "Don't leave. Tell me what to do," he begged, his voice riddled with desperation. "Stella, tell me. I'd trade places with you if I could. Please, for the life of me, I can't remember making any promise." Carl paused, saddened by the empty echo of his pitiful plea. Stella was gone. The moment was gone. And to Carl it felt like the truth of life itself had gone.

He propped a pillow behind him and the wall, crossed his arms over his massive chest, and waited for the dawn. At this stage of the miserable game, Carl didn't really care whether the sun ever rose again or not. Of course, the sun did rise, and for those keeping track on the calendar, it marked the dawn of Wednesday, July 22.

Although Emmet was prepared to be disappointed again, today was another day on which Contessa was scheduled to visit the farm. He hoped she would come, but it was a guarded hope. Emmet had a lot on his mind. When he and Warren had decided to rent Binkerton Town Hall, his exuberant optimism had blinded him to the details attached to launching a variety entertainment show. But now he was committed (so was Jimmy Aylor's money), and he was afraid he'd overestimated his own talents. That was a personal fear—as a performer. Thinking as a producer, Emmet knew the lineup was thin. At best he had forty minutes of material from which to create a ninety-minute show, and the more he anticipated the big night, the greater his anxiety.

By Wednesday morning at breakfast Emmet was a nervous wreck. He sat motionless at the kitchen table, glaring grimly at a glass of orange juice. He had no appetite. This was not the case with his partner. After polishing off two fried eggs, Warren hungrily attacked a bowl of cereal. Apropos of nothing, Emmet moaned and declared, "We've gotta find a singer."

Warren paused between spoonfuls. "That's the umpteenth time you've told me that."

"And I might say it again," Emmet said unapologetically. "We've got seventeen days before the curtain goes up, and I'm still trying to fill a hole in the middle of the show. Our show."

Warren replied in a flat, matter-of-fact tone, "I'd sing if I could, but I can't. As it is, I'm already risking my life on those stupid stilts."

Emmet shook his head despairingly. "Dad said we should let Angeline sing. He must think we're complete amateurs."

Warren dropped his spoon into the bowl and stared across the table. His patience was clearly strained. "I don't want to start an argument or anything, Emmet, but we *are* amateurs. We've never performed in front of an audience before."

Emmet frowned and retorted sharply, "Everyone has to start somewhere. Charlie Chaplin wasn't *born* on the stage. There's a real difference between inexperience and a child gurgling and gooing in front of a paying crowd."

Warren got up from his chair. He didn't feel pressured the way Emmet did. (The little anxiety he did feel was with regard to Holly. In the past three weeks she'd sent him two postcards, both informing him that a letter was on the way.) As he carried his bowl and plate to the sink, he advised Emmet, "Don't bark at me. We're in this together. I'm on your side, remember?"

Emmet slumped forward and leaned his head on the table. "I'm sorry, Warren, it's just that I want us to produce a winning show on opening night . . . not some rinky-dink fiasco."

"You mean flop, huh?" said Archibald, wandering in from the pantry. Although he didn't always succeed, Archibald was doing his best to remain discontented until Carl's problem was resolved.

"Whatever," Emmet allowed. The fight had gone out of him.

"I heard you talking."

"So?"

Archibald shrugged tentatively before informing Emmet, "It's probably not worth mentioning. I mean, he's not really with it these days. But I know a singer."

"Who?" Emmet asked, more doubtful than hopeful.

"I've never heard him myself . . . but Jimmy Aylor told me that Carl sings better than Frank Sinatra."

Emmet lifted his head and glared doubtfully at Archibald. Carl Plummers, a singer? The notion was simply too far-fetched for Emmet to take seriously.

Emmet sulked in the barn for most of the morning, but at twelve thirty-eight, when he saw Mike Cunningham's pickup at the gate, his mood improved dramatically. It kept improving as the truck approached, and by the time Emmet greeted Contessa in the parking lot, he was rather giddy. "Ah, gee," he said facetiously. "I was really hoping you'd bring Porcellina."

"You wouldn't hope I brought Porcellina if you had to feed her all day," Contessa noted with a quick smile.

"Probably not," Emmet agreed. "How about you? I can feed you something, if you want."

"No thanks. Maybe later. I'm here to work. We've got a ton of details to iron out if we're going to put on a good show."

Emmet gazed admiringly at Contessa. For the first time in weeks he felt encouraged as a producer. With Contessa at his side, the odds of success seemed to shift in his favor. "I love the way your mind works," he said sincerely.

Contessa accepted the compliment with minimal ado and gazed around the yard. "So, where do you keep your props? And where are Warren and Senator?"

Emmet gestured toward the barn.

Contessa started walking in a businesslike manner.

Part of Emmet wished to grab Contessa's hand and hold it while they walked, yet it was not his boldest part. As he rushed ahead to open the barn door for her, he said proudly, "We found a swing-band album that sounds great with our tumbling routine."

"That's good," Contessa remarked. "By the way, I've been working on a xylophone number to go with your juggling."

That pleased Emmet. "You have?"

"Yep," Contessa said with a knowing smile. "It's full of bings, tings, and trills for every time you drop a ball."

Emmet thought but did not say: Sure, I drop occasionally. There isn't a juggler in the world who doesn't.

While Contessa and the Unlikely Trio brainstormed in the barn, Matilda was in her bedroom twiddling her thumbs and peering idly out the window. Though it was early afternoon on a sunny day, she didn't know what to do with herself. After returning from the beach, Leopold had recalled the pages of his manuscript that he'd given her to edit and refused to give her any more. She'd had her fill of pleasure reading—last night she'd finished a curious novel about a boy named Thorpe who lived alone in a cave. Now, as much as Matilda hated to admit it, she was bored.

Matilda was embarrassed by boredom. She agreed with Leopold when he'd written that boredom was an excuse for not thinking.

She was trying to decide what she should think about when she happened to glimpse Archibald walking toward the front gate. She jumped up from her desk and scrambled downstairs. On her way outdoors she called to Goosebumps, "Wake up, you lazy mutt."

After Matilda caught up with her brother and learned that he was on his way to speak with Emma Bean, she decided to tag along. They followed the shadiest of the three paths that eventually led to the Hillacre estate, and when it delivered them to the banks of the Mataponi River, they plopped down for a rest. Actually, only Archibald and Matilda plopped down; Goosebumps ran forward and stood jowl deep in the refreshing water.

After a quiet spell Archibald rolled from his back to his stomach and asked Matilda, "Is Leopold's book exciting?"

"For some it might be," Matilda allowed. "It probably wouldn't excite you. There's no action scenes."

"No action? What's it good for then?"

"It's good for thinking about life and all the deep secrets that are hidden in the universe."

"Is it like the Bible?"

Matilda said with her eyes that she thought poorly of the question. "No. Not at all. Anyway, it's not a book for people to read. I doubt Leopold will ever finish writing it."

"I don't blame him, if it's not exciting," Archibald joked, then grew serious when he saw the pained look on Matilda's face. He knew the book was important to her. "Why won't he finish it?"

Matilda stuck a blade of grass between her two front teeth and paused to reflect before replying, "Leopold believes that he's getting old. I think he's afraid he won't have anything important to do if he finishes his book."

Archibald nodded with understanding. "I've noticed that people start acting strange when they get old."

"Yep," agreed Matilda. "And speaking of strange, what's the scoop on that pyramid thing in the carriage house?"

"What thing?" Archibald feigned ignorance.

"Don't *what thing* me," Matilda retorted. "I accidentally went in there last week and saw it under a tarp. I know you've been helping her build it, but I don't know what it is."

Archibald pulled off his shirt and wrapped it around his head. He was stalling for time.

"Arch. I touched it. I know it exists."

"It was a secret," Archibald said sharply. "But since you *accidentally* went snooping where you shouldn't have, I suppose I can tell you: It's an invention that doesn't work."

"Even so, what did Aunt Emma build it for?"

Archibald stood and turned to face the river. As he watched the water flow past Goosebumps, he thought about the two times that he'd tried to activate the Projector. The only thing he'd felt on the first attempt was a cramp where the swing pressed against his bottom. Although the second try had failed as well, it had at least been interesting. He'd fallen asleep and had a funny dream about Carl dancing in a field. Archibald shuddered as he thought of Carl: He was the reason Archibald had tried the Projector in the first place. It was on Carl's behalf that he wanted to visit the astral plane.

"Who knows what Aunt Emma had in mind when she designed the thing?" Archibald said over his shoulder to Matilda. "I only got interested in it because I wanted to help Carl remember something. Something very important that he forgot."

Matilda spit the blade of grass from her mouth. "Aha! It's a memory machine?"

Archibald laughed, skipped forward, and dove into the river. He surfaced, shook water from his hair, and told Matilda, "You might be right. I can't remember if it's a memory machine or not. Like I said, it doesn't work."

Later, when Archibald and Matilda arrived at the Hillacre estate, they found a note pinned to the kitchen door. It stated bluntly: "We're napping. Go away."

"They must be forming a new habit," observed Matilda. "This is the third time in two weeks I've seen that same note."

"Maybe it's the heat," suggested Archibald. "Want to wake them?"

"We'd better not," said Matilda, suddenly turning to Archibald with a devious glimmer in her eyes. "But if you don't mind, we can slip into the carriage house and have a good look at the memory machine."

Archibald shrugged. "Yeah, okay. No use making this trip for nothing."

That afternoon, in New York City, Marvin Jinks was sitting at his desk digesting a late lunch when his assistant informed him, "Mr. Slide wants to see you in his office."

Marvin gulped. "What does he want?"

"No idea," said Bijou. "You know Earl."

Marvin combed his hair and straightened his tie before wandering down the hall to see the boss. Marvin had been dreading a confrontation with Earl Slide ever since returning to New York without having signed Leopold Hillacre as a client. As Marvin tapped on the boss's door, he was expecting to be fired. Or worse.

"Sit down."

"Yes sir. Thank you," Marvin mumbled obsequiously.

Earl shuffled through some papers, then held up a letter. "I just wanted to congratulate you on your effort with that Hillacre fellow. Seems you made quite an impression."

"Sir?" Marvin could hardly believe his ears.

"He says here that his book is not quite ready, but he will contact us when it is. To be honest, I was afraid Moberg, Quinn might beat us out on this one."

"Yes. No. Not them." It took Marvin a moment to recover his composure. "I mean, may the best agency win."

"That's the attitude," said Earl. "You can go now. I just wanted to tell you to keep up the good work."

Marvin felt perkier than a new coffee pot as he sauntered back to his desk. He wouldn't be eating any books after all! He paused on his way past Bijou's desk and said with a wink, "Dinner on me tonight, if you're available."

Chapter Seventeen

When Holly awoke on Friday, July 24, she looked around at the impersonal decor of her room at Queen's Playland and moaned. This was her thirty-third morning away from home, and the thrill of costarring in the Wild West show was beginning to wane. She was doing what she had always wanted to do . . . yet somehow the reality of the experience didn't measure up to the magnificence of her dreams. Her days started slow, dragged on tediously while she waited for show time, then ended in lazy evenings at the apartment with Flea. Thank goodness for Flea, Holly mused. I'd be nuts without her. But then Holly thought: I'm keeping Flea from Garland. She can hardly wait until next week when she switches places with Bellamonte.

Holly rolled out of bed, got dressed, and sat at the little table in the corner of her room. The wastebasket by the chair was full of crumpled paper. Her pen lay on a clean notepad, exactly where she'd left it the night before. She picked up the pen, and for the fifteenth time in as many days, she started a letter to Warren: "Dear Warren, There is no excuse for this letter's long delay. I don't know what holds me back. It is surely not a lack of feelings for you. They brew in my heart like a storm. Sometimes, when I'm alone, I can hear your voice in my head. You warn me to be careful, or ask how I'm doing, or just say hello. It doesn't matter what you say, Warren, I'm happy when I hear your voice." Here Holly paused to shake her wrist and stretch her legs. While she was up, she decided to take a shower.

After drying off and dressing again, she sat down to read what she had written. Not too bad, she thought. Not bad at all. She picked up her pen, leaned over the pad, and then— like the day before, and a spate of days before that one—her hand grew mysteriously stiff and her mind went steamroller flat. Why, why, why can't I write this letter? she wondered.

Five minutes later Holly heard Flea stirring in the kitchen, and a minute after that she set her pen down and went to have breakfast. Although Holly normally dwelled on the glories of this world and gave little credence to the next, she was beginning to wonder if an interfering spirit was working to keep her letter unwritten. It was a spooky thought . . . but something was stopping her. Something wouldn't let her communicate with Warren. She could feel it.

As the day wore on, Holly's sense of distraction grew, and she found herself feeling increasingly confused. Try though she did, she could not figure out what was bothering her. Whatever it was, it was persistent. Indeed, the only clear moments she had during the day occurred when she went to saddle Dan before the show. For some reason saddling Dan felt natural to her and she experienced a brief respite of normalcy. It did not last. By the time she and Dan arrived at the staging point behind the arena gate, Holly was feeling strange and disoriented again. A sort of muffled alarm went off in her head when the rest of the cast greeted her as if everything was just fine. Didn't they sense what she sensed? Didn't they feel her foreboding?

In the next instant Sally Swope signaled for the gate to open, and Holly had no more time to be confused. She nudged Dan's flanks and they pranced into the arena. Halfway through their introductory loop she was performing a routine side-switch maneuver when she fell.

Holly knew when she hit the ground that her leg was broken. She heard it snap. Even she was amazed by the way she reacted. In spite of the pain, she laughed. She couldn't bend her leg or stand up, but at least her mind was clear. The strange feeling that had plagued her all day was gone.

Holly was rushed by ambulance to Memorial Hospital in Richmond, where an orthopedic surgeon set her leg in a full-length cast. Flea rode with Holly and stayed at her side throughout the evening and the night.

Late the next morning when Holly left the hospital with Clementine and Henry, Flea waved good-bye to them through the window of the ground-floor visitors' lobby. Flea was waiting for Garland. He had kindly offered to drive to Richmond, pick her up, drive to Queen's Playland and put Dan in his trailer while she packed her and Holly's personal belongings, then drive her home. Now that's a real gentleman, thought Flea.

· · ·

Archibald, Matilda, Emmet, Goosebumps, and Senator were in the backyard when Clementine and Henry returned to the farm with Holly at midday. Angeline was inside with Bellamonte, who had volunteered to "watch the younguns as long as necessary." Warren was hiding in the barn. He wanted to wait until the hoopla died down before speaking with Holly. He watched from the window in the tool room as Henry parked his truck and helped his injured daughter into the house. Before entering through the back door, Holly paused on her crutches and turned her eyes toward the barn. Warren was gripped with sudden anxiety. It appeared as though she was looking right at him, and she clearly wasn't pleased. Indeed, she seemed mad.

Warren drew back from the window and berated himself for being so uptight. I'm a Southerner now, he reminded himself. I should have welcomed Holly home with a bouquet of flowers. That's the kind of gesture that would have pleased her.

Archibald joined the rest of the crowd that gathered around Holly in the parlor, but he wasn't feeling very social. He was busy constructing a fresh theory about Emma's invention. His theory had been unwittingly sparked by Matilda when he showed her the Projector. Although she'd believed she was looking at a memory machine, she had wondered aloud (just as Leopold had speculated with Emma) whether the contraption was similar to Emma's prize carpet, the power of which was linked to the phases of the moon.

Archibald was aware that the carpet flew only at sunset on a new moon. He also knew there was no logical connection between the carpet and the Projector. Even so, he was desperate to help Carl and he figured he had nothing to lose by investigating the possibilities. After signing Holly's cast, he excused himself from the house and headed to Aylor's Store. The moon would be full tonight. He wanted to prepare Carl.

Matilda took note of Archibald's departure and assumed he was up to something fishy. (That was a standard assumption with Archibald.) She reminded herself to grill him later.

As Emmet listened to Holly and Henry discuss the accident clause in her contract, the thought of so much money reminded him that he had a show to prepare. Before leaving the parlor, he told Holly, "Don't worry, you'll walk again one day."

"Oh, Emmet," Holly said in a sweet voice. "Would you spread some fresh straw in Dan's stall and make sure he has water and oats when Garland brings him home?"

It was one of those family-farming duties that Emmet was glad to perform. "Sure. I'll fix him up."

"Thank you," said Holly, adding quickly, "And if you see that sidekick of yours, tell him I'm home and I'd like to have a word with him."

There was a newfound confidence in Emmet's step as he walked to the barn. It had been there since Wednesday, when Contessa had put her stamp on the show. After finding solutions to problems Emmet hadn't known existed, she'd introduced a number of quality components to the production. One improvement she provided (free of charge) was the addition of her father's act. As Emmet had been elated to hear, Mike Cunningham had once worked off-Broadway as a magician. Having an experienced hand like Mike in the lineup did much to improve Emmet's outlook. Although he wasn't all that pleased when Contessa endorsed Henry's notion of putting Angeline on stage, he figured it was a fair trade for Mike and he agreed to give his baby sister a try. Contessa had also pointed out that ten-foot stilts were fine for circus tents or outdoor festivals, but inappropriate for the stage. "His head will be lost in the rafters," she had noted clinically.

"What should we do?" Emmet had asked.

"Cut them down, or make a placard so Warren can walk around Binkerton and advertise the show."

"I'll cut them down," Warren had volunteered before Emmet had a chance to consider using him as a promotional tool.

That was fine with Contessa, except for one hitch. "Warren has to wear long trousers. The appeal of stilts is that they create the illusion of a tall person. Without the right pants, Warren will just look like a guy walking on sticks."

"Where are we going to find extra-long pants?"

"Make them" was Contessa's reply.

Emmet now found Warren on the floor of the tool room, securing a pair of boots to the tips of his shortened stilts. "Holly wants to see you pronto."

"She does?" Warren seemed surprised.

"Of course she does, you idiot. Get in there."

Warren returned the screwdriver to Henry's toolbox and removed the broom from its hook. Emmet snatched it from Warren's hand and ordered, "Go. I'll sweep up."

When Warren entered the parlor, he found Holly sitting with Angeline, Clementine, and Bellamonte. He greeted the two older women with a nervous smile, then gestured hello to Holly and plopped awkwardly down on the sofa.

Clementine caught Bellamonte's eye and nodded toward the kitchen. Then she stooped to pick up Angeline and said for Warren's benefit, "It's time for someone we know to have her diaper changed."

Warren gazed appreciatively at Clementine, then slowly

turned to Holly. Much to his vast relief she flashed him a tender look that contained no visible traces of anger. Her voice matched her expression as she said, "Nice to see you again, Warren. I owe you an apology for the letter I never wrote."

"Oh no you don't," Warren replied quickly. "I'm sure the show kept you too busy to write."

"That's nice for you to say, but still, I owe you an apology," Holly countered. "I offered to send you a letter and I never did. I did try to write one, but for some reason it wouldn't come out. So anyway, I apologize for not doing what I said I would. As close as we are, it's important we do what we tell each other we are going to do."

Warren's heart soared. Holly was making it obvious that she valued their relationship. Before he could think of a response, she resumed speaking. "What I was trying to say in the letter, but couldn't, was . . ." Holly paused while she adjusted the cushion under her cast.

"Need a hand?" Warren leaned forward on the sofa.

"Thank you, I'm fine," Holly said in a voice rich with warmth. (Although Warren never suspected as much, Holly's mood had been medically enhanced by the painkillers the doctor had given her.) "So, as I wanted to say in the letter I never wrote, I didn't realize it until I went away and met some other people, but now I know that the day Aunt Emma brought you to the farm was the luckiest day of my life."

Warren arose from the sofa and went to take one of Holly's hands in his. Never one for too many words, he gazed adoringly into Holly's eyes and told her, "It was a lucky day for me, too."

• • •

When Archibald strode into Aylor's Store and headed down the center aisle, he was relieved to see that Carl was awake. "I want to talk," he stated flatly as he hopped onto the flour barrel.

Carl acknowledged him with a raised eyebrow.

Archibald focused a deeply determined, unflinching gaze at Carl. The look did not waver when he spoke. "Listen, Carl, I've had enough of this misery. I know you feel bad about your sister. For whatever it's worth, so do I. But the time has come for us to deal with the situation."

Lines of distress rippled across Carl's forehead. "I'm ready to deal with it, Arch . . . and I would if I knew how."

"Remember I told you I had something cooking?"

"Yes."

"I've got a plan," said Archibald, dropping to the floor and crossing to stand beside Carl. After a cautious look around, Archibald whispered, "Tonight when the moon is at its fullest, I want you to try to reach Stella and tell her to look for me."

Carl blinked uncomprehendingly. "How? In my dreams?"

"Any way you can."

"And if I do, which I doubt because I've tried and failed too many times, where do you want me to tell her to look for you? Down here . . . or up there?"

"Up there. If things work out tonight, I'm going up to the astral plane when the moon is full."

Carl blinked again. "Do you know what you're saying? I mean, you're still alive, Arch. Stella's been dead over thirty years."

Archibald was not in the mood to debate details. "It doesn't matter. Dead or alive, the soul is only a vibration."

Carl hung his head. He was too ashamed to tell Archibald

that Stella had recently faded away forever. He felt somehow responsible for losing her twice. "I'll try it, Arch. And let's say I get lucky. Exactly what do you want me to say?"

Except where his jaw quivered with tension, Archibald showed no sign of emotion. "Just tell Stella to look for me."

"That's it?"

"That's it," Archibald instructed. "Wait until the moon is at its brightest, then start thinking of her and thinking of me. Do it real hard, Carl. Think as strong as you can."

Carl nodded. "I will. Just remember, you promised you wouldn't do anything dangerous."

"I'll be fine," Archibald said bravely.

Chapter Eighteen

Before joining the family at dinner that evening, Archibald fished a long-sleeved black shirt and a pair of dark brown pants out of storage and slid them under his cot in the pantry. He had already hidden a navy-blue stocking cap beneath his pillow.

The Dithers were digging into dessert when Garland and Flea arrived on the farm with Dan in tow. Considering the long day they'd had, they were in surprisingly good spirits. Of course, they said yes to pie. Afterward Emmet went to the barn to feed Dan, and Warren went upstairs to pack his clothes. When Warren returned with his suitcase, Clementine sent Matilda to change the sheets on his bed, then told Archibald, "I thank you for letting Warren use your space. That was generous of you. It's yours again now. You can move out of the pantry."

Archibald tensed. He had not anticipated Warren's departure when making plans for tonight's full moon. He smiled innocently at his mother and said, "Being generous is fun. You know me, I'll do anything to help the family. And hey, what the heck! I think I'll stay on the cot for one more night. Let Emmet have some privacy for a change."

When Matilda, who was already suspicious, discovered that Archibald had volunteered to remain in the pantry for an extra night, she knew for certain that he was up to something devious. After supper she followed him out to the porch and announced that she smelled a rat.

Archibald pretended to sniff at the air.

Matilda smirked and sat on the swing beside her younger brother. "You think you can fool me."

"What?"

Matilda kicked the swing into motion. "I'm not dense. You're up to something."

Archibald frowned. It was tough growing up with a detective for a sister. "Okay, I admit it. I'm planning to start a band. You know, like the Beatles."

Matilda wasn't fooled, but she wanted him to think she was, so she went along with his game. "What instrument will you play?"

Archibald was shrewd enough to know that he had not thrown Matilda off his trail, and that she would probably continue to watch him. Nevertheless, he continued with his bluff. "I'll probably play drums. Maybe the trumpet."

"Cool. You kind of look like Ringo."

"Yeah, yeah, yeah. I'll have to grow my hair long."

As usual, Clementine was the last person to go to bed that night. Matilda was listening as Clementine finished brushing her teeth and retired to the master bedroom. Matilda was wearing long pants and a T-shirt under her pajamas. She checked the clock by her bed and decided to wait another ten minutes before tiptoeing downstairs to look in on Archibald. If her mother or father awoke and caught her in the house, she planned to tell them she was worried about Holly. Because of her cast, Holly was sleeping on the sofa in the parlor.

Archibald had an ear cocked for the telltale creak of Matilda sneaking downstairs. He waited patiently. Soon, just as he expected, the third step from the bottom announced Matilda's descent.

Matilda eased across the darkened kitchen and peeked into the pantry. Moonlight streamed through the rear door and she could see Archibald sprawled on the cot with his face buried in a pillow. He snored lightly. Matilda stepped back and glanced at the illuminated clock over the stove. It was five past eleven. She watched and waited for ten minutes. Archibald shifted once and adjusted his pillow; it seemed like a normal sleeping move. Twice he cleared congestion from his throat.

Matilda waited eight more minutes. Slowly, bit by bit, she began to doubt her original suspicions about Archibald. She could usually trust her hunches, but like anyone and everyone, she knew they were sometimes wrong. She yawned, waited three minutes more, then made her way stealthily back to bed.

Ten seconds after Archibald heard the step creak he pulled his pants on over his shorts. Ten seconds later he headed out the back door. There was no time to waste. Midnight approached.

In the best of conditions it was possible for Archibald to run from Dither Farm to the Hillacre estate in twenty-eight minutes. Tonight he made the trip in thirty-three, arriving at his destination at five minutes and forty seconds before twelve. As he stole across the lawn he noticed that the carriage-house doors were open. He was not alarmed—the big double doors were often left open. Still, some instinct bid him to exercise caution. He slunk into the shadows of the privet hedges to his left and approached the building in a circumspect manner.

Drat, he thought as he looked inside, relieved that the word hadn't escaped his mouth. A candle was burning on a plate in front of the Astral Projector and his great-aunt Emma was sitting in the swing. Her thumbs touched the tips of her respective middle fingers, and Archibald wasn't sure, but he thought he heard her humming.

He backed into the hedges and lay with his arms crossed under his chin. He would have to wait his turn. Fortunately the swamp mosquitoes didn't know Archibald was there.

He could not remember drifting off, nor did he know how long he had slept when he awoke, but when he crawled out from under the hedge, the candle had been extinguished or taken away. He turned to the main house. An upstairs window was yellowed by lamp light. Although Archibald had no way of knowing so, Emma and Leopold were propped up in their canopied bed, commiserating over Emma's failed experiment. Considering all the planning and work she had put into her project, Emma was rather relaxed about her defeat. After all, as Leopold pointed out, her carpet had flown and she had done wonders with the Zandinski Box, which gave her a two-out-of-three experimental success rate. "That kind of record would make any alchemist proud."

"Yes, I suppose," Emma agreed with a sigh as she switched off the light. Already in the back of her mind she was developing an idea for a Psychosensory Enhancement Booth.

Archibald stepped through the coils of wire surrounding the Projector and settled in the swing. Although he couldn't see the moon when he looked up, he could see its light twinkling through the crystal above. He drew a deep breath, rested his chin on his chest, and concentrated on clearing his mind. It wasn't easily cleared. He kept wondering if Carl was awake and thinking, and if so, had he been able to reach Stella?

Archibald willed himself to forget everything. It was time to let his mind go free.

The moment stretched out before him. He could hear an owl hooting on the far side of Weeping Willow Swamp. He absorbed the sound as one absorbs familiar music. The tip of his nose itched, so he scratched it. Time passed.

He called the old photograph into his mind and concentrated on the image of Carl's sister.

More time passed and he started to forget where he was. His willpower began to fade. He was beginning to float . . . upward.

Was this a dream?

He saw cows munching on clouds. His mother rummaging in a basket. A porpoise smiled, its teeth gleaming in an orderly row. Acorn popped out of the water and handed Archibald a cup of coffee. As Archibald looked at the liquid in the cup, it swirled off the rim with a whooshing sound. Archibald could feel himself moving sideways. He was gliding. No, dancing. Each step carried him a thousand yards.

Who was he dancing with?

Shy laughter. *Who are you?* he asked the girl he was dancing with. She was leading him across the sky. Her hair flew back and he saw it was Stella.

Archibald tried to speak and ask her what promise Carl had made, but his voice stuck in his belly. He struggled. Finally he opened his mouth. His lips were shaped like a trumpet. The sky exploded with colors.

Stella was gone, and Archibald was sitting in a tree by a placid lake. An owl on a limb looked down at him and blinked.

Archibald heard a familiar voice. The owl spread its wings and disappeared. He heard the voice again. "Archibald. Wake up. It's after four in the morning."

He opened his eyes and saw Matilda.

"I figured I'd find you here."

"What?" Archibald's mind was torn in two directions. He was straining to remember his dream—his projection, or whatever had happened—and at the same time he was grappling with the fact that Matilda was standing in the carriage house.

She laughed and explained. "I knew you were up to something, so about a half hour ago I checked in the pantry. When I saw you were gone, I guessed you were here."

"Why'd you come?" Archibald asked sleepily as he got out of the swing and stepped carefully between coils of wire.

"Just curious," Matilda said simply. "And you should be glad I found you before the sun rises. You'd be in serious trouble if Dad got up for breakfast and found you missing."

Archibald shook his head. He was awake now. "Matilda, you'd be in trouble too."

"Yes, and that's why we should go now. Come on, you can tell me everything on the way home."

"I will, but later," Archibald agreed. "I'm not speaking right now. You'll have to wait until tomorrow."

And indeed, although Matilda pestered him to talk on several occasions, Archibald did not utter a single word on the hurried journey home. He spent the time reviewing the rapidly fading images that had passed through his mind while sitting in the Astral Projector.

Was it a dream? Or did I project? Did I really dance with Stella?

Chapter Nineteen

Henry had worked all week with Wade Butcher before driving to Richmond on Saturday to pick Holly up from the hospital. By nighttime he was especially tired and went to bed early. He slept later than usual on Sunday morning. It wasn't until almost seven thirty that he went down to the kitchen.

When Henry looked in the coffee can, it was all but empty, so he reached into the pantry for a backup. There was Archibald, dead asleep on the cot. Henry smiled and thought: It's a marvel how well that rascal has behaved this summer. So far he hasn't been embroiled in a single fiasco. Maybe, just maybe, the boy is starting to mature.

Emmet awoke with a start at eight thirty on Sunday morning. Without having to count, he knew he had fourteen more days to prepare for the big show. That included today, which was special. It was the date upon which he and Contessa had agreed to begin their promotional blitz. Their budget was zero and their plan was simple. They would use homemade posters. Each would be brightly colored and highly original (some radically so), yet all would deliver the same message. Below lies a facsimile that does not catch the visual flavor of the hand-painted original.

❧ VAUDEVILLE ISN'T DEAD ☜

Variety entertainment for families and single people

---

seven-thirty Saturday August 8
Binkerton Town Hall
adults $5 kids $3 babies free

Starring:
The Unlikely Trio
Emmet Dither, Warren Robinson, and Senator,
the world's smartest lower primate

Costarring:
Contessa Cunningham and her dancing pig

Special guest appearances by:
Mike the Amazing,
Alice the Accordion Woman,
and Angeline the Operatic Infant

COME JOIN THE FUN ITS A BARGAIN

By Emmet's bed there were seven posters: one for the window at Aylor's Store, and six for each of the other businesses in Willow County that carried Clementine's Cider.

Contessa had made eight posters: three for King County, two for her father to put up in Bricksburg, two for Binkerton, and one that Sheriff Ludwell Newton had agreed to hang in his office. Up for reelection in November, he was being indiscreetly nice to almost everybody.

Holly was awake and ready for breakfast when Clementine brought it to her at nine thirty. Holly ate slowly. She had time to kill before half past noon, when she intended to call Warren. (Her mother's edict about visiting neighbors on Sundays applied to the telephone as well.) Although Holly really just wanted to hear Warren's voice, her pretext for phoning was to get his measurements. She had volunteered to make the long-legged pants he needed for his stilts. She knew the length he needed—forty inches—but she wasn't sure about the circumference of his waist.

Matilda was in the kitchen by ten. While she was waiting for her toast to pop, she peeked in the pantry and chuckled. This was no acting job: Archibald was asleep. She considered rousing him to hear the explanation he owed her, but then kindly decided to be patient. He had to wake up eventually.

Archibald opened his eyes at eleven fifteen, yet did not stir from his position. He had woken up thinking about what had happened the night before. He couldn't decide if he had actually projected or had just had a dream. It was a strange dream, if that's what it was. But how could he know? It was probably a dream. That's what it felt like . . . except for those huge, giant sideways steps across the sky. He remembered them as real. Then it hit him: Oh, no! Stella! How am I going to tell Carl I saw her but didn't ask about his promise?

Archibald suddenly realized he was hungry. He hopped off the cot, pulled on his red shorts, and went to the kitchen. He needed a hot, greasy breakfast before heading to Aylor's Store and facing Carl.

Matilda and Goosebumps were waiting outside when he left the house. "Good afternoon, Mr. Van Winkle," Matilda teased. "Ready to give me the scoop on last night?"

"Ugh," Archibald groaned. He had eaten too fast.

"That was no answer," noted Matilda.

"It's all you're getting right now," Archibald said as he started toward the gate. When Matilda and Goosebumps followed on his heels, he snapped, "I'm going to see Carl about something personal."

"You can talk while we walk."

"Grrr."

"Grrr yourself," retorted Matilda, passing through the gate ahead of Archibald. "I'm not letting you worm out of this."

Archibald followed Goosebumps through the gate, which he slammed behind him before telling Matilda, "You can come with me, but no questions until after I speak with Carl."

Matilda threw back her head and laughed. For some reason she was extremely tickled by the whole situation.

It was half past past noon when the trio left the woods and cut through a cornfield to Aylor's Store. As they approached the parking lot, they could hear a strange huffing sound. Neither Matilda nor Archibald could imagine what was making the sound, nor could they easily believe it when they saw what it was. They halted simultaneously at the edge of the field: There was Carl Plummer wearing gray stretch pants, a gray sweatshirt, and a pair of blue size-twelve tennis shoes. Incredibly, he was doing jumping jacks.

Archibald and Matilda were stunned. So was Goosebumps. They stood riveted in place. Eventually Archibald found his voice and called, "Carl, what are you doing?"

Carl halted his motion and smiled. "What does it look like I'm doing?"

"Exercising?" Matilda guessed.

"That's right," Carl said happily, then bent and pointed vaguely at his toes.

Archibald was dumbfounded. The Carl he saw before him was not the man he'd been worrying about all summer.

Carl stretched his arms, then rested his hands on his hips and remarked to Archibald, "You seem surprised by something."

Of all the millions of facial reactions that have taken place throughout the history of the world, the expression that now appeared on Archibald's was unprecedented. "Carl, what can I say? I never expected to find you outside hopping around like you were on fire."

Carl grinned and wiped sweat from his brow. "So, Arch, how'd your experiment go last night?"

"That's what I want to know," adjoined Matilda.

Archibald continued to stare incredulously at Carl. "Forget my experiment. It was nothing. What happened to you?"

Carl added a wink to his grin, then nodded over his shoulder toward the store. "Let's go in. I'll buy you a soda. I don't want to overdo things on my first day."

"Your first day of what?" Archibald demanded as he rushed to Carl's side.

"Yeah. What's this all about?" asked Matilda.

Carl paused on the store steps long enough to answer, "This is my first day of fulfilling a promise I made over thirty years ago."

Archibald froze. "You found her? She told you?"

"No. I just remembered."

Archibald was trembling with anticipation as he followed

Carl into the store. "Carl, what was it? What did you remember?"

"Excuse me," Matilda interjected, "but I still don't know what you two are talking about."

Carl stood with his back to the checkout counter and leaned casually on his elbows. "It's a long story, Matilda," he said with a thoughtful air. "Years ago I made a promise that I forgot. It bothered me that I couldn't remember, but then last night it all came back to me. So now I feel much better."

"Oh," said Matilda. She knew it was only a partial answer, but she was satisfied for the moment.

Archibald wasn't anywhere near satisfied. The suspense was driving him mad. "*What?*" he shouted.

Carl smiled warmly at Archibald and explained, "At midnight I started thinking real hard, just like you told me. I wasn't getting anywhere. I didn't feel like I was making a connection with Stella or anything, but I'd given you my word, so I kept thinking. After a while I heard an owl hooting in the distance. I don't know why, but the sound of that owl made me happy. Then suddenly it all came back to me. One night at the orphanage Stella woke me up and made me swear something. She was very serious about it. I had to cross my heart and hope to die if I didn't do it. It seems strange, now that I remember. . . . Anyway, when I made my vow, we heard an owl hooting outside the orphanage. It startled us and we both laughed nervously." Carl paused and mused privately for a moment. Whatever he was thinking, it obviously brought him joy.

Archibald was ready to burst with curiosity. "What did you promise?"

Carl chuckled. "It was simple, really. She made me swear

that if we ever got separated, I wouldn't be sad and I'd learn to be happy without her."

Archibald staggered over and leaned against the magazine rack. "That's it? You swore you wouldn't be sad?"

Carl nodded. "Yep. I promised to be happy no matter what happened to us. I'm sure glad I remembered."

Archibald didn't know what to think. He descended slowly to the floor and sat with his head hanging forward.

"Who was Stella?" asked Matilda.

"She was my sister," Carl said matter-of-factly. He lifted a hand and pointed across the store at the cooler. "Go fetch us some sodas. It looks like Archibald needs a root beer fast."

Chapter Twenty

"Only the best for Warren," Holly asserted as she examined the swatches in the catalogue Bellamonte Smoot had brought to the house. Holly was flush with unspent income from Queen's Playland and she could afford to put money where her mouth was. Her choice was made the instant she saw the square of crushed velvet. "I'll have a bolt of that."

"The dark green?" Bellamonte checked to be sure.

"Yes, thank you."

"An excellent selection," said Bellamonte. "What size bolt? How many yards of fabric do you need?"

"Oh, make it seven," said Holly. "Someone we know might get married soon, and if they do, I'll be needing a new dress for the wedding."

Bellamonte clucked softly to herself. She and everyone else in the neighborhood was excited by the rumor that Garland Barlow had gone jewelry shopping in Bricksburg. She flipped to the rear of the catalogue and pointed to an illustration. "Would you like some white lace to go with the velvet?"

Holly glanced quickly at the book. "I'd rather have pink, please. And, Bellamonte, I appreciate you doing this for me."

With a bit of uncredited assistance from Clementine, Holly managed to complete Warren's pants in time for the "Vaudeville Isn't Dead" dress rehearsal on Thursday, August 6. Warren was effusively thankful. The pants were constructed with a vertical zipper in the back of each leg. "Absolutely perfect. Holly, you're a gem. It'll be easy getting in and out of these. I don't know how to thank you enough."

Holly was anything but demure. With a knowing (and somewhat suggestive) smile, she pointed to one of her blushing cheeks.

Warren bent to do her bidding. He did not falter when Holly quickly turned her face and offered a pair of puckered lips instead of a cheek. It wasn't the lengthiest kiss in the world, but it wasn't the briefest, either.

When Emmet arrived at Binkerton Town Hall on Thursday evening, Eugenna White was there to meet them with a key. She was also carrying an invoice for forty dollars. She handed it to Emmet and explained that their original rental agreement had not included a rehearsal night. Jimmy Aylor was carrying Alice's accordion into the lobby at that moment and happened to overhear Eugenna. He allowed her to drone on about insurance, utilities, and other nonsense, then stepped forward and gave her a piece of his mind. Good ol' Jimmy. He expressed himself so pointedly that Eugenna not only withdrew her bill, she apologized for having submitted it in the first place.

It was due in large part to Mike Cunningham that the

rehearsal was productive. Of course, Mike's expertise would have been worthless if Emmet had not been wise enough to accept his advice. Emmet was no egotist; he handed the director's reins to the experienced showman and stepped gratefully into the ranks. As a result, by the end of the evening the troupe had learned what to expect from each other when. With their timing cues established, they proceeded to resolve a slew of technical difficulties and polish their entrances and exits.

Granted, there was a snafu or two—such as Porcellina's tendency to squeal when Alice played the accordion—that didn't get ironed out, but they were minor drawbacks. On the plus side, Angeline surprised everyone with her professionalism. When Henry put her on stage, she curtsied like her mother had taught her, sang a beautiful little melody, then bowed and jumped into her father's arms. Also on a positive note, Jimmy Aylor was drafted as a front man. He agreed to warm up the crowd with a few jokes and introduce the show. And there was Rosey, whose presence in the wings had a beneficial effect on Senator's performance. Prior to tonight's rehearsal Senator had shown a marked lack of enthusiasm for practice, but with Rosey watching, he turned single flips into doubles, double flips into triples, and imbued every one of his gestures with high drama. It was an astounding display of primate energy. Later, after the rehearsal was over, Emmet's parting words to Mike were, "Whatever you do, don't forget to bring Rosey on Saturday night."

At noontime on Friday, Flea Jenfries stopped by Dither Farm wearing a diamond the size of a peanut. Although the news of her betrothal to Garland was expected, it didn't dampen

Clementine's response. She threw her arms around her little friend, danced an impromptu jig, and cried, "I couldn't imagine being happier for anyone I know."

"Thank you," Flea chirped as she bobbed up and down with Clementine, then added in a confidential whisper, "he wants to start having children right away."

"I bet he does," Clementine giggled, releasing the bride to be and stepping back to admire her glow.

Flea grinned and grinned.

"When is the big day?"

"Next Saturday."

"That soon! Next Saturday?"

"That's right. One week from tomorrow. He wanted to elope last night, but I convinced him to wait."

"Good Lord, Flea. That doesn't give us much time to prepare."

Flea blushed happily. "I know, but what can I do, he wants to start a family right away."

For Emmet, the eighth of August was divided into five parts. First was morning—an optimistic time, during which he reflected proudly on all he had achieved. This was followed by midday—a busy period spent gathering props and chatting with Warren. Then came the afternoon phase—when Emmet was assaulted by so many doubts, he wished he'd never heard of vaudeville. And there was early evening—an exhilarating hour when all he could think of was a curtain opening.

Finally, the fifth and most intense phase of the day found Emmet with his ear pressed against the stage curtain—beyond which he heard the scuffing and tapping of heels on the wooden floor, the creaking of metal chairs, and the buzz of convivial voices calling hello across the room. Unable to resist the urge, he peeked into the auditorium. Henry was in the front row holding Angeline in his lap. (Henry would wait until Jimmy flashed a signal, then hoist his daughter up onto the stage.) Clementine sat on Henry's left. Next to her was Holly. At the end of the row Emmet saw Archibald sitting with a nattily attired Carl Plummers. Although still twice as hefty as most men, Carl was slimmer than he had been in a decade. Tonight Carl was wearing a starched white shirt, a black bow tie, gray slacks, and shiny new loafers. Emmet thought he looked fabulous. Two rows behind Carl, Matilda sat next to Emma and Leopold. Beside them were Flea and Garland. As Emmet watched, Acorn and Bart ushered Millie Ross to a seat in the fourth row.

Emmet conservatively guessed that a third of the two hundred available seats were occupied. Had he not been so nervous, he would have been relieved by the profitable turnout. And paying customers continued to trickle through the door.

Emmet jumped when Contessa snuck up behind him and whispered in his ear, "Break a leg."

Emmet whirled around. "What's that supposed to mean?"

Contessa explained, "In the theater, it's bad luck to say good luck. So instead you say break a leg."

"I didn't know that." Emmet was obviously relieved. "In that case, I hope you break every bone in your body."

"Thanks," said Contessa. "You too."

Emmet grinned, then gulped and stood rigid. It was show time: Jimmy Aylor walked out in front of the curtain and greeted the crowd with a wave.

"Ready backstage," called Mike Cunningham.

Jimmy thanked everyone for coming, promised them a

terrific show, then stepped back through the curtain and nodded to Alice. It was her cue to create mood music. Ten seconds later Warren entered the auditorium on his stilts. He dipped low through the main entrance and began making his way toward the stage. Several children called to him as he proceeded down the center aisle, but he pretended not to see or hear anyone. He appeared to be looking for something he could not find. When he reached the steps at stage right, he paused and put a hand to his chin. The curtain parted. A light brightened on stage. Emmet and Senator were bent over a steamer trunk.

Emmet and Senator rummaged through the trunk as Warren ascended the steps and crossed to center stage. They showed no sign of knowing that Warren was behind them. Emmet withdrew a doll from the trunk and tossed it over his shoulder. Warren, feigning surprise, caught the doll. Then Senator threw a grapefruit over his shoulder. Warren caught that as well, and stuffed the doll into one of the deep pockets in his pants. When Emmet hurled a shoe, Warren stuffed the grapefruit in a pocket and caught the shoe. Senator waved a hairbrush in the air. Warren went wide-eyed with worry, stuffed the shoe in a pocket, and grabbed the flying hairbrush out of the air. Then came a kitchen mitt . . . a wooden spoon . . . and finally Emmet withdrew a hatchet from the trunk and held it up for inspection. It was a rubber toy, but Warren pretended otherwise. He grimaced and raced off stage as fast as his stilts would carry him. There was a roar of laughter, followed by an explosion of applause.

Emmet was filled with joy. The first act was a hit. The stage lights pulsated. As he exchanged the hatchet for juggling balls, Contessa rolled her xylophone into view and Senator dragged the trunk offstage. Although Emmet's juggling routine was meant to be a demonstration of physical dexterity, the audience seemed to think it was a comedy act. This erroneous perception was no doubt enhanced by Contessa, who pinged and tinged on the xylophone without taking her eyes off the rotating balls. When Emmet missed a catch, she thunked a low note as the ball hit the stage floor. The audience guffawed as one. Emmet knew a good thing when he heard it. An instant later he dropped two balls at once. Thunk, plunk. Another explosion of laughter. Emmet wasn't proud; he went with the laughs. By the time he bowed at the end of his routine, he had adopted the demeanor of a clown.

"Looks like we killed them," Emmet whispered as he joined Warren backstage.

"Yeah, they seem to love us," Warren agreed without removing his gaze from Porcellina's dance, or prance . . . or whatever it was that she was doing.

Warren was right. The audience did love them, as they demonstrated when Angeline was put on the stage. She started perfectly, with a curtsey, but then was so startled by the applause that she stepped backward and seemed to forget that she was supposed to sing. Henry whispered encouragement to her, but still she hesitated and looked around. The audience was utterly charmed and broke into renewed applause. Angeline smiled when they did this, then bowed and ran to the front of the stage. Henry moved quickly and caught her when she jumped. He turned with Angeline to face the crowd and blushed proudly as they gave a standing ovation.

Next the blindfolded ring-toss routine garnered a polite round of applause for Emmet and Senator. Alice Aylor followed with her accordion and played "When the Saints Come

Marching In." Although the applause was brief and soft, it was respectful. As Emma whispered slyly to Leopold, "Maybe Alice should take up painting or one of the other quiet arts."

The crowd grew perfectly silent when Mike Cunningham took the stage and made a rope stand on end. They remained spellbound as he pulled a rabbit out of his hat, then made a quart of water disappear into a folded newspaper. Most of the people from Willow County were the type to believe what they saw, and many of them had a hard time reconciling their vision with their intellectual understanding of the world. To put it mildly, they were dazzled by Mike's wizardry.

After the curtain closed on Mike, Jimmy stepped forward and announced, "Now for the stars of our show, the Unlikely Trio."

As Emmet and Warren tumbled onstage, they were afraid that Senator might not join them. Indeed, the distracted monkey missed his cue by three seconds. Finally, though, he tore himself away from Rosey and bounded backward into the limelight. With a squeal he sprang onto Warren's head. Senator stood tall for a second before Warren grabbed his paws and swung him in a wide arc. At the end of the arc Warren released Senator, who turned a triple flip before landing on his feet at center stage. This was just an opening gambit. It was followed by a rapid sequence of physically impressive, well-choreographed stunts that held the audience enthralled.

Chapter Twenty-one

Emmet was filled with a kind of wild, untamed joy as he led the troupe out for a curtain call. What more could he want? The show was a success. His fellow performers (except for Angeline, who had fallen asleep) were as rapturous as he was. Contessa's hand was in his. Even Rosey had come out to stand beside Senator. Emmet had never smiled wider in his whole life.

Someone called for an encore. The call was seconded . . . then a dozen voices joined the chorus: "Encore! Encore!"

Emmet saw Archibald signaling for his attention. Contessa saw him too and quickly grasped his intentions. She whispered to Emmet, "He wants Carl to sing the encore."

Emmet hesitated for an instant, then pointed at Archibald and mouthed, "Bring him up."

Archibald turned and shook a finger at Carl. "Listen, pal.

You nearly ruined my summer. So you owe me. No arguments. Get up there and sing us a song."

Carl smiled, patted Archibald on the head, and turned toward the stage steps. The crowd saw what was happening and began to murmur with anticipation. As Carl lumbered on stage, the other performers edged back and formed a semicircle behind him.

While Carl waited for the murmuring to subside, Leopold leaned sideways and whispered in Matilda's ear, "Will you remember something for me?"

Matilda nodded that she would.

"It's for my book. Remind me later that I said: True heroes shelter whole communities in their hearts. When the hero suffers, the people are sad. When the hero is happy, everyone is free."

"That's it?" Matilda inquired dubiously.

"Yes. It's more profound than you think."

Carl coughed and a hush fell over the Town Hall. His palms turned upward and his arms lifted slowly in front of him. Then he began to sing, in a voice that grew in power and volume as the song took over:

> Well . . . I looked over Jordan
> And what did I see
> Coming for to carry me home?
> T'was a band of angels
> Coming after me,
> Coming for to carry me home.
> Swing low,
> Sweet chariot
> Coming for to carry me home.

Swing low,
Sweet chariot
Coming for to carry me home.

It was a performance that no one would ever forget. By the end of the song everyone in the building was wailing the lyrics at the top of their lungs. Bart was so inspired, he uttered his first declarative statement in recent history: "Carl sure can sing up a storm!"

Indeed he could sing. For the next five years in Willow County, whenever anyone got slightly depressed, someone would mention Carl's performance and the ailing person's spirits improved immediately.

The evening ended with an uproarious cheer. The house lights came on and people began to file from the auditorium. Somewhat reluctantly, Emmet let go of Contessa's hand.

"This is for tomorrow," she said, surprising him with a kiss on his cheek. "Happy birthday."

"How'd you know?"

Contessa didn't say anything. Instead she surprised Emmet with another kiss on his other cheek.

Emmet didn't know what to do or say—he just knew he wanted Contessa to surprise him forever. Out of the corner of his eye he saw Warren leap from the stage and rush to assist Holly with her crutches. Emmet had no way of guessing what Holly was telling Warren, but he could tell from the look on Warren's face that she must have said something promising and sweet.